EDWARD'S CHOICE

A NOVEL

BY JONATHAN YOUNG

Sinner

I'm sure that I was born without sin; *that* came later. At the start I was just flesh and bones - a mind and a heart - like anybody else.

But very soon sin crept up on me. Though I don't really remember how, sin came and then came again like it was destined to always be there. Sometimes, in my bleakest moments, it felt like I – Edward Hill – was so immersed in sin, that it couldn't ever be washed away.

I used to think about judgement day and God's methodology for deciding who went upstairs and who went down - *gnashing of teeth* and all that. The theory I feared the most was something I labelled the 'godliness queue.' In this system, every man and woman would take their place in the line to heaven based on how free of sin their lives have been, with bonus points earned for work towards sharing the 'good news.'

I'd imagine a busy scene, with great missionaries and church leaders striding confidently to the front - closely followed by the most pious parishioners, such as the army of willing old ladies I've observed serving tea after church service each Sunday. Less desirable characters, of course, would skulk to the back, already fearing their fate.

And when, after a while, the line settled into its final order and the shuffling stopped, God would arrive to confirm what this fate would be. Walking along from the front and counting each person as He passed, He would eventually stop about half way down to declare to the world:

"That's it. Heaven has no more room,"

And for those beyond that point - that would be that.

But where would I be? As I've thought about this, I've often considered whether I'd make the cut. Am I nearer the back than the front? Have I earned my place in heaven? Or have I actually done more of the Devil's work?

Whisper it quietly. I've often been afraid of the answer.

Please don't think that my intention is to sensationalise my sins. I know Christians who wear their previous sinful lives like proud badges - 'cheat,' 'thief,' 'adulterer' – as if having dined at the Devil's table and still been saved, they have somehow achieved a cool and 'experienced' status to be revered by other believers with less colourful pasts. I guess my own sins have often monopolised my thoughts because of their almost routine occurrence rather than any nostalgic desire to hang onto them as souvenirs.

Yet because of their constancy, there have been times when life has felt like wading through thick mud, rather than striding confidently to the front of a queue.

But who decreed that I spend much of my life shackled by the weight of my mistakes? Who's keeping track? Who, at our lowest moments reminds us that our sin is perpetual, inevitable, and irreversible?

I'm here to tell you...not Him upstairs. Not in the sense of translating our file of bad behaviour into diversions or time penalties that must be taken on the journey to His door. I'm also here to tell you that if, like me, you still have times when you feel like you're wading, maybe you have not quite got your head around God's greatest gift.

I'm still working on it. He's been working on me and this is my story.

Edward's Choice

The tendency to view my Christian life like some sin and righteousness bank account, somehow took a hold of me through my early life. It wasn't a value system that I could trace to any particular event, but certain things that happen can act like landmarks to show you just how lost you have become.

As a seventeen year old I was invited by Sam Herring, my best friend at the time, to join him and his family on a weekend away at a holiday village in Wales. I had the sort of relaxed and good humoured relationship with Sam's mom and dad that you would not think of having with your own parents, and I also got on well with his brother Charles, who was not too proud to hang around with us despite being two years older.

Part of the reason for having me along was possibly to add momentum to Sam and Charles' case to escape the other family members as much as they could, but the weekend began in a way that undermined this logic. We spent the first evening dutifully playing charades and various board games with the rest, and it was only really on the second night that we managed to cut-loose from the chalet, in the hope of discovering some entertainment more appropriate for boys of our age.

The Disco bar that we found probably matched our expectations of what this would be, even if we knew Sam's parents would disapprove. Charles was happy to stay there and even buy us drinks, believing that Sam and I could normally be relied upon not to do anything too crazy.

Under normal circumstances, he would have been right. You could not in any way describe us as rebels or troublemakers. Sam was a fellow member of a church youth group, and although slightly roguish at times, was basically a good kid. Certainly, given the range of people generally available to befriend at that age, he was the sort of boy that parents would gently encourage you to spend time with, rather than secretly wish you would ditch.

Similarly, I was not in the business of intentionally doing the wrong thing. Like him however, I had a normal sense of mischief and an appetite to do pretty much whatever was necessary for them to declare their weekend 'good fun' once we had returned home.

At this age, the basis for much of this was chatting-up girls. Unfortunately, on this night, our fairly feeble efforts in this respect met with the failure they deserved. Charles led us in talking to three older-looking girls we had earlier spotted in the resort's swimming complex, and in his muddled hurry to find something interesting to say, began complimenting one of the girls on the swimming costume she had been wearing. It came across as predictably creepy, and from then on it was only a matter of time before we were brushed off. Sam tried willfully to recover the situation, exercising at least some of the tact and smooth-talking that his elder brother lacked, but moments later, the hardly apologetic, "we have to go now" arrived.

About the same time we had begun to attract a few suspicious glances from the bar staff anyway, and fearing a set of questions and consequences that could lead back to Sam's parents, we decided to cut our losses and leave.

It was on that journey back, and specifically when we decided to 'borrow' some mountain bikes that we found unchained outside, that the true horror of the night would creep up. This in itself, was purely opportunistic, and something we fully intended to atone for the following morning when they would be returned to the same place. However, as if to demonstrate how wrongdoing and sin can proliferate, they would take us to much more significant trouble.

It all began predictably. Each one of us showing off with a jump, wheelie, or other trick, as the fresh air seemed to exaggerate the affects of what we had drank. And before long, our contest turned to seeing who could ride the quickest.

"Idiot," I remember Sam crying at one point, as his brother almost collided with his back wheel.

We swerved in and out of shadowy, foreboding trees, crisscrossing the dimly lit path back to the chalet.

But before we could make it back and save ourselves, the darkness would close in. As we swerved around one particular bend, I noticed someone moving on the path ahead: a dark crooked figure, stuttering along, then still. The man there was clearly drunk — perhaps someone from the bar trying to find his accommodation, or a tramp who had wandered in from the nearby village.

What happened next will forever be clouded in the chaos and irrationality of those moments, no matter how I've tried to make sense of the memories. There was shouting. Maybe even some laughter. And after two or three minutes we were gone. But that time was enough for us to unfathomably circle the man on our bicycles several times, scaring him beyond reason. And enough time for him to become convinced we might attack. Though we didn't mean to do this in a threatening manner - though hurting him definitely wasn't our intention, he pirouetted nervously on the spot, as if assessing how he might escape, before leaping over the fence at the side of the path. It was an irrational act with a potentially dangerous outcome. At the other side of the boundary was a steep bank of around fifteen feet, which he tumbled down into the dark below.

We fled as quickly as we could, not stopping to check if he was okay, and not daring to consider he might be hurt, injured, or worse.

As I've made clear, I have never reflected positively upon any sin, but the thought of what I had done offended me immediately. I could not even begin to rationalise what had motivated me to get involved in these moments of madness, aside from some fleeting sense of amusement. I found my actions as mindless and embarrassing then, as I do now.

I knew it would go on to cost me sleep. Although fuelled by 'alcohol,' I couldn't get away from the fact, I had actually chosen to be the author of that person's fear. There *was* momentary sport in what we had done.

Not a word of it was spoken between us in the following days. It was as if discussing it might cement the memories into our collective reality - though I suspect that the others, like me, may have visited the bottom of the bank to confirm he wasn't still lying there. Other than that, we ritualistically played-out our weekend's activities as if nothing had happened. But while our immediate sense of fear eased, the longer time passed without us hearing rumours of anyone being found within the site, I knew the uncomfortable images and thoughts of what we had done didn't leave any of us.

For me, they bled into almost every hour. And the strange thing was, I found myself wanting to keep them all close to me; a reel of hurt until my true punishment was delivered.

So the process began. For a few days I went on forcing myself to think about what I had done, especially as I lay alone in my bed; awaking angrily on several occasions, when I realized my tiredness had overcome me. I stopped myself doing most of the things I really wanted to do, or spending time with people I liked. Indirectly, I even hoped for bad news, or to be the victim of unkindness. These and other forms of penalty were delivered upon me, with the objective of demonstrating to God my guilt and regret, until the bank account felt like it was in credit again. Until this particular overdraft was paid-off, long after the weekend itself had ebbed away.

To a greater or lesser extent, this was the pattern I'd follow almost every time I was guilty of sin that I felt warranted this type of self-loathing and penalty: mocking other kids that were overweight or for whatever other reason an 'easy target,' deceiving my parents about where I was and what I was doing – selfishness, stealing, fighting, spitting. All these things I did once or many times. And in turn, each one was offset against either my self-imposed punishment or other setbacks that would follow, such as poor exam results or a bad sequence of results for my football team. Self-deprivation or disappointment followed sin as part of the constant clamour for balance to be retained. For a long time this was my life - the life of Edward Hill.

That was until I realized I could break free. Until I became aware that my ability to be forgiven was reliant upon my willingness to truly accept that this gift had already been granted. For someone who had routinely asked God's forgiveness for all manner of sins from an early age, simply because I had been taught to, it really did take a long time for this particular penny to drop. In fact, about ten months after the unfortunate events I have described. Ironically, this was also at a time when my attendance at church or anything related to Christianity had become rare.

It was not as if my faith in 'God' as a force in my life had been shaken. By now I considered myself a Christian and no matter how far I slipped, I realized that deep down my life would always be anchored back to Him. It was more a case that I felt the particular messages I heard at the church youth group were becoming less relevant and somehow less audible to me. Sitting through some of the meetings had become like listening to a poorly tuned radio. There were meaningful words to be heard, but these had become muddled with a variety of competing sounds, voices, and static from life outside. Eventually, trying to hear through the distortion seemed like such an effort that I gave in and stopped attending altogether.

I had also become tired of discovering fresh ways to clear my conscience. My sin mountain had grown beyond sight and somehow I felt more at ease with people who clearly, often unashamedly, had sin spilling across their lives too.

But one afternoon I had received a call.

"Ed, you have got to come."

Although inexplicably I had not spoken to Sam in several weeks, he clearly did not have time to make any apologies for this, or even hear mine.

"They're coming from right across the county and you know what that means don't you?" The words were said with infectious excitement, "*Socialising*, my friend; Socialising with good Christian people that we don't even know today."

He was talking about a combined church event for teenagers of all Christian denominations within the area, at a nearby leisure centre, and what he actually meant was that this was an opportunity to meet new girls.

For him, this type of 'socialising' had always been one of the big draws of attending our church youth group. Clearly there was ample opportunity to meet girls back at school, and more recently at college, or pubs and discos, but here the environment seemed far less competitive. The unique nature of this meeting made it an even more promising prospect. He simply must be there, even if he too had attended our own group's meetings infrequently as of late.

"C'mon man, it'll be a half-hour for the bible bashing bit, and then there's a social," he urged me. "It'll be great to catch up with everyone, and besides, its high-time you got yourself a girlfriend."

Although on one level, the fact I shared Sam's 'lost sheep' status made me a natural choice for a companion, I liked to think he had genuinely missed hanging around with me over the previous weeks. I had certainly missed him. There was something about Sam's enthusiasm that always dragged you with him, and this, coupled with the fact I had very little else planned-out for that evening, made me more than happy to fulfil my role in his plans on this occasion.

"I'll pick you up at seven-fifteen," he said. It was done.

Sam was predictably punctual, but unfortunately the traffic through town did not share his sense of urgency, and by the time we arrived everyone in the room had their heads bowed, as the speaker led the group in an initial prayer. It was also clear as we awkwardly made our way across the hall that Sam's expectations regarding all the new people the event might draw, would prove groundless. Despite the period I'd been away, I still recognized most of the faces. Nonetheless, we soon found the safety of two seats at a careful distance from the temporarily erected podium.

Following two hymns that both Sam and I apathetically mimed our way through, we again sat down as the guy at the front began to address the group.

There wasn't a great deal that stuck in my mind about him based on that night, aside from the fact he looked fairly well dressed compared to some of the preachers you would see on the church youth group circuit. Most would either go for something loud, like a Hawaiian shirt, absurdly assuming this would score points with *the youngsters*, or at the other extreme, turn up in the same dandruff speckled blazers they had worn for all their speaking appointments for many years. This chap, however, had on fashionable jeans and a T-shirt beneath a suit jacket – and though middle-aged, gave the impression he had that 'cool uncle' quality that so few middle-aged men achieve.

He also spoke in a style that was relaxed and easy, but still arresting. Much more significantly though, he clearly had something important to say. Whereas normally I could slip off into a daydream that would typically last all the way through a half-hour sermon, here the words seemed to hone in on me; they demanded my attention. My casual interest was transformed into something more fixed and I found myself waiting for the next sentence to arrive.

Essentially he was talking about our relationship with God. He began by simply stating that His love was already ours. He also reaffirmed that God's forgiveness had also been granted. What stirred me in this was his challenge as to the part we must play in this exchange. We could not simply be passive in receipt of these gifts, he argued. Rather, we must acknowledge this with our faith and believe it was given. To judge His forgiveness as something we could choose to accept or not, or impose our own worldly parameters upon, was a fundamental misinterpretation of Christianity itself.

He went on to use scripture from Mark's gospel (later recounted in Luke), describing when Jesus Himself was challenged by the scribes and the Pharisees as to why He ate with tax collectors and sinners. Was it *appropriate*, they implied, that this great prophet, the Holy One of God gave His time to such undesirables? How had they earned this in comparison to more righteous men? His answer was unambiguous.

"Those who are well have no need of a physician, but those who are sick. I did not come to call *the* righteous, but sinners, to repentance" (Mark 2:17).

On this basis, he angrily rejected the idea of a Christian life being about carefully balancing scales of good and bad, holiness and transgression. This was a view, he suggested, that the Devil peddled, to create confusion and guilt in our minds.

By now I was engrossed – transfixed. I knew straight away that these were the chaotic thoughts I had experienced. Indeed, this all seemed uncannily constructed to expose and defeat the very demons that had begun to plague me. Could it be that I had been wrong about my debt of sin?

Increasingly, the physical reality of the meeting, the room and the people, had all become irrelevant. There was no distortion on this occasion: just his words. As far as I was concerned this was God himself, talking to me.

"For the Son of Man did not come to destroy men's lives but to save them" (Luke 9:56).

It dawned upon me that I had begun to believe something almost opposite to this. But He had set about unpacking the hurt within my heart.

I also began to realize what an unattractive and dangerous version of Christianity I had subscribed to recently. My increasingly gloomy beliefs painted a scenario of 'man the sinner' having to deal with, or 'make up for,' what has past before even earning an audience with God. For many people, including myself over recent months, the notion of ever achieving this became a more and more hopeless prospect. In the end it seemed almost impossible to even talk to Him. It was the credit card bill that nobody would dare open.

Except that the guy standing at the front of the room was now telling me that I had got it wrong; that others who also felt they had sinned beyond recovery had got it wrong. In fact, Jesus knew that the debtor who is forgiven the most, will come to love Him the most (Luke 7:41-42).

He could be found among the frail, the sick, the tormented, and *the sinners;* because they were the very ones He came to save. From the time He began His teachings to the moment He was crucified, *they* were the ones Jesus sought out.

Afterwards, I sat for a few moments, wondering whether others had been moved by that half hour of 'bible bashing' in the same way that I had. *I was torn between laughing out loud out of relief, and sobbing.* But as friends began to gather together and the sound of chat and laughter rippled around the room, I assumed that for most, the preacher's words had not carried the same relevance as they had for me. Or, like me, they had decided to suppress their emotions, feeling understandably concerned about what others might think if they did not. Even in this environment, behaviour viewed as too 'religious' or otherwise odd could be seen as strange.

Of the people I knew there, only a girl called Trudy – one of the leaders from the old youth group – possibly noticed my response. She had only really started helping out there at the point when my own attendance was becoming less reliable, but she seemed more disturbed than most about my steady disaffection – perhaps because she was only two or three years my senior. Tonight, she simply came up to me, put her hand on my shoulder and gave a knowing and tender smile that seemed to say, 'I understand – I'm thrilled for you.'

Although for Sam's sake, I did mingle and talk to a few other people during the rest of the evening, in truth, I lacked any conviction in doing this. My thoughts were still rooted in what I had heard earlier, and I was glad when he finally gave me the sign that he was ready to leave.

For Sam, the night had not been the limitless opportunity to collect girls' phone numbers that he had envisaged. But despite this, he was in good spirits in the car on the journey back.

"You know what mate," he said, as intently as I had heard him speak before, "I'm going to give them (the church youth group) another go. I'm going to go back."

He kept his eyes fixed on the road, as every now and then, the glare of approaching cars gleamed against his face, revealing a subtle but determined smile that seemed somehow new.

It was a statement that did not require any response or support, but I simply answered, "Good. I'm pleased." Just for those brief seconds, it was like I'd caught a glimpse of another Sam – a Sam behind the outgoing and captivating persona that everyone found so likeable. It was far too easy to make lazy, over-simplified assumptions based on the part of him you would normally see. It occurred to me that perhaps, to some extent, he too had been affected by what he heard tonight. Maybe his lack of disappointment as we made our way home was a clue that his motivation for the whole evening had actually been more to do with him rediscovering the group, than the reasons he argued initially. I hoped so.

For my part, I had not necessarily gone there to hear such life changing words, but that evening I travelled home with an optimism that I had not felt for a while. I was content.

I did not quite know whether going back to the same group was the answer for me, but I did feel reassured that my spiritual journey would continue one way or another. In many ways this was an endpoint for me – I knew I was saved.

Unfortunately by this stage, the choices that I had made about how I would live my Christian life, also meant that it would inevitably stray off course again.

There have been long periods since, when I've slipped back into the mode of living that is characterised by 'fear' of retribution, or agitatedly trying to amend for my sin. It is difficult not to think of the many elements that make up life as rewards or punishments. On one hand you have the simple pleasures of a memorable day or holiday, time with people you love, or the many other triggers that can invite happiness in. On the other, there is a bad day at school or work, failure, illness, loss, and disappointment. When things have gone well - periods of sustained happiness – my temptation has still often been to look for signs that my run was about to end, because I cannot always believe that my behaviour has justified such a good deal in life.

But that night taught me that it was not God who would have me view my 'lot' in these terms. Despite all that has happened since - no matter how engulfed I have become in the world and its prohibitive values - thinking back to that night reminds me that in His eyes we are all as precious and pure as babies — free of sin. Free of the cycle of cause and effect, regurgitated over and over again.

There will be no queue on judgement day. Heaven does not have a maximum capacity. You just have to hold on to faith and keep walking towards Him. This is the story of my walk.

Inflatable Ring

Of course, you have to take the first step somewhere. For most Christians this is a moment - a blessing from above - that remains with them forever.

Mine was unforgettable.

I remember the chorus of a hymn recycling over and over in my mind, and the warmth of the sun upon me — exaggerated by a few degrees by the glass panels above. I remember thinking that until then, I hadn't really appreciated all my deficiencies. I was topped up in a way that I never thought possible or necessary. I was perfectly still, but floating; I was floating across the surface of God's earth.

So even when echoing voices nearby reminded me where I was, they could not deprive me of this experience. Though I briefly wondered if it might all seem inconsequential to someone looking down from on high, I knew that to Him I was somehow pivotal.

I could be sure about these things, because great things had happened that night. Fragments of heaven had fallen to earth. Stirring testimonies, profound blessings and God's presence had provided undeniable evidence of His love, if it were needed. So much so, that I thought to myself, surely those who had doubted now worshiped?

As if sensing my question, a nearby voice entered my bubble of contentment:

"She'll come around. You know she'll come around mate."

This was how it was for me - several years earlier - when I came to realize that God's gaze was fixed upon *my* soul. This was my moment of discovery, as I slowly rotated upon an inflatable ring, in a swimming pool.

But those words and the mere mention of *her* seemed to drag me with the world, turning away from this brief juxtaposition with heaven. This is what she had seemed so capable of doing in the short time I had known her. She could remind me in an instant of my worldliness.

My moment had passed.

"I think..." I hesitated, unprepared for the interruption or its poignancy, "I mean, you're right. It's like she's scared of what it will mean, but she'll come around - just maybe not this week."

It occurred to me then: what if some people never experience *that* feeling? What if they just go on waiting — looking up at the sky and growing more frustrated that their miracle doesn't arrive?

The voice belonged to David Stone. We had met for the first time only six days before but had effortlessly become good friends in the time since. I liked his relaxed manner and the fact he seemed to have a maturity and acumen that was absent in the rest of us. He also had a constant capacity for astute and witty observations and his commentary had become a welcome reference point for the events of the last week.

Right now we were enjoying a relaxing swim in the pool at Hathernwray Hall. This had become our ritual after the 'worship' meeting each night.

'Hathernwray' is a beautiful nineteenth century mansion set on the edge of the Cotswolds and had been our home during the previous week.

Why we and the other residents were there depended on your point of view. This was either a place where Christians gathered to have fun and find fellowship under the banner of their faith, *or* it was a hideaway - a safe haven from the realities of the real world. The former was what I imaged my parents had hoped when they first suggested I spend a week of my summer holidays there, while the latter pretty accurately reflected the opinions of one Clara Downing. Clara was the girl David had referred to.

As well as David and me, around eight other teenagers from our local area had boarded a train destined for the southwest the previous Saturday. I had met a few of them before, and was aware that most had relatives that attended the same church as my parents, but I did not really count any of them as friends at that stage.

I have since heard it said that *the Church* sometimes lacks creativity in its strategies to attract young people through its doors, but this was possibly a local exception. We were all in our mid-teens and approaching what was rightly perceived to be a pressurized life-stage. Rather than sit by and watch us struggle to disseminate the myriad of worldly influences that would help shape our adolescent personalities, our parents and relatives probably sought a plan that would at least help to provide sensible companionship during this time. In pushing us together, it was hoped that friendships would form and that the group itself could evolve into something more lasting around a Christian theme.

It was probably an ambitious vision. Although we all came from roughly the same background and area, we had not so much chosen each other as been chosen *for* each other. Yet, it was quickly clear that the result would be more positive than they could ever have hoped. Rather than resist the circumstances for being false or over-engineered, we bonded in a way that even then suggested a mandate for us to continue beyond that week.

I knew almost immediately that people like David, and Sam Herring, who was also on the trip, would become more lasting friends.

Edward's Choice

From day one, we found every aspect satisfying and enjoyable. Together with the other groups from around the country, we all excitedly feasted on getting to know each other and our new society seemed to gel right away. The busy program of activities and games that were organized by the leaders there, was a perfect platform for this. We probably took it for granted at the time, but even on the first day, a communal tour around the hall's grounds gave us an early opportunity to get to know some of the others, as well as filling the hours before the first worship meeting that afternoon.

But it was later, after the meeting, when we discovered the place where most of our spare time would be blissfully wasted away.

We had wandered into the room which adjoined the dimly lit library almost by accident, having idly followed a group of other kids heading in the direction after dinner. But within minutes we were caught up in the magical atmosphere that could always be found there. Dotingly cupping warm drinks in their hands, people hung around on the large sofas and armchairs – and just talked.

"Is this the first Christian holiday you've been on?" someone asked. "It is for me, and I'll be honest, I'm petrified."

Very soon, we were part of those conversations too.

We talked about Hathernwray - our hopes and our fears - and also about things back home. It felt sophisticated, almost like we were playing at being adults. From that point on, it was as if we were liberated to really share the substance and values of our lives and have people truly listen.

In one sense Clara was right - we were safe. It was as if the common room hierarchy, the social posturing and the conventions that could be so inhibiting at school were all happily missing here. At times I had found myself bound by, and even pedaling the 'schoolyard code,' but my inclination was to quietly resist it. Here wearing the right clothes or using the latest teenage slang did not matter. It was exciting but also slightly frightening. I knew that I had to be *real*.

At the core of this, David, Sam and I quickly formed an uncomplicated but promising friendship. Anyone who has been part of a group like that, knows that at the time you just don't stop to consider why things are clicking so well, but we went on to spend so many happy hours together, where the banter and laughter, and eventually trust between us, seemed to arrive without any effort. We began doing most things together, but equally, were not in anyway possessive of each other in respect to spending time with other people we met during the week.

In part, this was probably because many of the other people we met there were girls. It was clear straightway that Hathernwray offered much to our teenage curiosity around the opposite sex, and Sam was typically the most forward in meeting this opportunity with action.

David and I enjoyed his audacious and brash attempts to introduce himself, such as one morning at breakfast, when he left us to join a large group of girls at a nearby table. Though it was initially difficult to listen in to any of their conversation from where we were, as we passed on our way out, we overheard him saying:

"Listen, thanks for letting me join you because normally I'm painfully shy with this sort of thing.

So, which one of you is going to challenge me to a game of tennis later?"

A few hours later, I was equally taken aback and slightly in awe, when I spotted one of the girls from that same group walk up to Sam and begin hugging him in a way that suggested a much greater familiarity between them. Noticing me from over her shoulder, he shrugged and whispered, "she took pity on me for being homesick – what can you do?"

Although David and I perhaps considered ourselves more sophisticated in our approach, like most teenagers we enjoyed having this sort of friend around. He was quickly and effectively breaking the ice with everyone we encountered.

And from his point of view, this assured confidence combined with his disarming smile meant that his reception was far from negative. Even after a day or two, most people would eagerly ask after him whenever David or I would turn up anywhere alone. And by the end of the holiday, at least five girls had approached Sam with slips of paper containing their addresses, pleading with him to write to them when he returned home.

If girls were an obvious reason why Hathernwray was instantly appealing to us, a less anticipated engagement was also developing around the Christian message that the institution was founded to deliver. Of course, we understood the religious context of Hathernwray, but I was expecting this manifest as no more than inconvenient 'Sunday School' type interruptions to our fun. It turned out to be something much more.

As I have alluded, given my upbringing I had been surrounded from an early age by notions of an Almighty God. I was familiar with many of the Bible stories on a superficial level; particularly those which stood out to me as fun or quirky like that of Jonah and the great fish, or for other reasons slightly more challenging, like the testing of Abraham's faith with his son Isaac. I knew from the New Testament that God sent His Son, Jesus Christ, to earth, so that our sins might be forgiven. The thing was that until now, I perceived that all these things were intended for the collective human race rather than me specifically. I could not see how I could lay claim to one of God's teachings any more than I could argue that one of His raindrops was actually sent to earth for me, despite the fact it may land upon my head.

During this week at Hathernwray, I would come to understand that God would disperse the clouds in order to warm *my* soul with His revitalizing sun. He would do it just for me. I would go as far as to say, that it was here that I truly began to understand my life could be something special.

It was a realization that crept up on me even during those first couple of days. Certain prayers spoken by the leaders, or hymns that would be sung, stuck in my mind and I felt like I had questions that I needed answering. And to my surprise the unique atmosphere of praise and awakening within the worship meetings seemed to break out into our conversations elsewhere as well.

I was both embarrassed and strangely excited by the social amnesty on talking about God. Even compared to church groups I attended later, there was a notable freedom in this respect. Hearing other kids speak about how new and frightening this all seemed, helped me come to terms with my feelings. It provided a platform for this period of discovery and helped build the stirring I felt inside.

Amid all this, Clara was a stubborn and lonely island. While others were openly moved by the journey of enlightenment they had begun, she remained impenetrable, proud, intriguing, and above all else, a committed atheist.

Like everybody there, I had become aware of her from the moment we arrived. She was attractive with stunning strawberry blonde hair and the sort of confident posture that, male or female, instantly made you uncomfortable with yourself. She had a magnetic quality that made people want to be with her, but was also somehow standoffish to the point that she would not initially seem to allow anyone to monopolize her time. Rumors quickly spread that she would openly and bullishly state that all this 'God stuff' was 'nonsense.'

My first opportunity to talk to her was during an outing to a boating lake in the nearby town that was again, organized by the youth group leaders. By now many of the residents simply joined in with whichever pastime was proposed, such was the sense of involvement and belonging that was developing.

Once there, around thirty people ventured out onto the water, splitting into groups of three or four per vessel, each taking turns to row with large wooden awes.

Following some understandable caution initially, the confidence of all the crews on the lake seemed to grow and some good humored splashing and semi-accidental collisions signaled the start of a more competitive period. From a fairly chaotic beginning, a full blooded game soon evolved whereby two teams of boats attempted to make it across to the opponents' side of the lake without being impeded, or even capsized by an enemy crew.

Clara was on board one of the opposition boats. I found out later that she was annoyed at how a pleasant afternoon's activity deteriorated into this unnecessary contest, but it was clear to me that she was a significant factor in the game for the two boys who accompanied her. Although they were clearly eager to triumph over us, their cautious maneuvering suggested that keeping her out of harms way — and dry - took precedence over any other objective.

For us too, she somehow assumed a pivotal role merely by the fact she was on the water. We immediately made her boat our priority, heading to cut them off by a small island.

Before long we were exchanging a few splashes with them. I am sure they would have retreated if they could, but we had occupied their route and there was no way past. With neither of us able to change momentum, we quickly reached a point when a collision was inevitable.

To a chorus of loud shouts and crackling laughter, our boats soon thudded together. Straight away, Sam was on his feet embroiled in a good hearted wrestle with an opponent at the point where the two crafts temporarily adjoined. The outcome was predictable - both boys, still clinging to each other's wrists, crashed into the dark water. David, a cunning tactician, then goaded the other boy that he dare not come aboard, and watched as he all too readily activated this trap. As he leapt across, David swiftly propelled the boat away at his end by pushing the awe against the bottom of the lake, leaving the poor chap to follow the other two into the cold.

I saw my opportunity and jumped across in the other direction, before the gap between us became too wide at my end as well.

My landing was safe enough, if a little ungraceful, and soon I was the captain of this new boat, with my one passenger still safely aboard. David hurriedly rowed away the other, towards his victory.

Clara sat like a spoiled princess, exposed, let down, and embarrassed by the stupidity of her guardsmen. Clearly caring little for who was in charge as long as she got back to the jetty, she poked an oar towards me.

"You can take me back if you like?" she directed.

Although not typically blessed with any real speed of thought or wit, I was mindful that someone who compelled people to notice her in the way she did, could perhaps only be stirred by indifference. I therefore decided to move against expectation.

"Actually, I'm pretty tired, would you mind?"

A reluctant smile broke onto Clara's face and almost immediately I knew I had sparked her interest. Amazingly she took the awes and began to move the boat steadily away.

"A real gentleman. Just my luck," she said sarcastically. "What's your name anyway?"

On the basis of this single event, and those few words, I had been chosen. It started with us simply going down to dinner together that evening, having chatted for most of the journey back from the lake. However, I would soon find Clara waiting for me after the meetings each morning, assuming that my time could be dedicated to her. Before long, we were almost routinely together during most of the ensuing days. While other boys were kept playfully close to her, I had been awarded the status of her favorite, for the remainder of the holiday. And for a while, I was a willing recipient of this honor.

I was to learn a lot more about Clara during that time: the fact she had spent years yo-yoing between addresses, given the breakdown of her parents' marriage and her own behavior which quickly became intolerable to different relatives; that she had been expelled from two private schools for being similarly unwilling to respond to their rules and expectations. She even shared details of her many relationships with members of the opposite sex, which she insisted, included a teacher at one of those schools. I had no reason to doubt any of it was true, and although she was only one year older than me, her life experience seemed to eclipse mine to an unbelievable extent.

And yet despite this, most of all, Clara gave the impression that she was bored with her life. She was waiting - waiting for something better, and all this was just filling the time until her fortunes would somehow dramatically change. She could not describe exactly what this would be or how it would happen, but she had an unwavering sense that the world owed her more. *I* was just helping her fill the time.

For my part, my interest in her wasn't driven by any real romantic aspirations, or for that matter, teenage lust. I *was* flattered by her interest, but for me it was much more about intrigue. She was feisty, opinionated, and argumentative. She stood out as being different and was prepared to challenge the views of the majority. In some ways there was something as admirable about her strength in voicing non-belief in this overtly Christian environment, as those who might risk the mockery of the majority when they openly proclaim their faith at school or in the workplace.

Our conversations were often good fun, but equally hard work on other occasions. Sometimes I suspected that she was conditioning me with her point of view so that I might be her defendant to the rest of the Hathernwray Hall community. On others, it was clear that I was being isolated from everybody else so that I might represent Christianity itself in an argument or debate she felt like having.

Questions on things like creation, sin, sex, lies, and death were all fired at me even though she knew that I was ill equipped to answer. These more often resulted in answers or conclusions that were unsatisfactory to either of us.

A good example occurred one day as we played chess on a giant board built into the courtyard at the front of the main hall. For me, this was merely a means to lazily enjoy the sunshine and Clara's company. I had no real strategy or resolve to win, especially given that I barely knew the rules of the game. However, she was in no mood to entertain my apathy. Her probing started almost as soon as she picked up the knee high Pawn to make her first move.

"Prove to me that there's a God."

"I can't," I replied, trying to dismiss the question.

"Why not?" she said.

"Well, I just can't."

I was on the back foot immediately.

She grinned broadly, acknowledging our shared appreciation that it was another argument we could not hope to resolve.

"If you can't, then how can you be so sure?"

"About what?"

"About this? she continued. "How can you justify what these people do every day?"

I couldn't answer.

For a moment, Clara somehow misinterpreted my silence as a quiet confidence - that I felt no need to respond. My pause was a threatening move that must be quashed immediately.

"How can anyone here be so sure that it isn't all just religious fervor, hysteria, or Mumbo-jumbo?" she said, her voice quickening.

The truth was that I didn't know. Although I felt I should, I had no answer, and what she said began to disturb me. These were obvious arguments that I could not instantly dismiss and it made me feel weak and slightly confused.

"Seriously, if there's no proof, then there's no substance. And if there's no substance, there's no point."

She took my knight with her queen.

At this moment, as she stood at the edge of the board waiting for my next move, more than any other time, she seemed so strong and beautiful. I wanted this stupid argument to end, and for her to stop pounding me with these questions. I wanted Clara to put an end to this. But still I answered.

"I think…" I paused, scratching around for a way out, "well, I think there *is* substance — lots of it — maybe too much to ever solve the argument."

"What do you mean?" she asked.

"Well, just look around you. Surely *this* is all substance. You know - those trees, the grass, even that old building — everything. It's all substance. But not just the external things, the people here as well."

Clara was quiet now.

"I guess what I'm saying is that His reflection is everywhere — it's in everything — in people's eyes. But there are so many places to look, you just can't pin it down."

Although still apprehensive, I began to feel encouraged by where my thought process was taking me.

I continued, "If you want proof, whether its all God or something else, I can't help thinking there's always gonna be gaps. *He* just didn't go around carving His initials into the things He created just to prove that they are His. Isn't the point that all these things were His, but that He gave them to us — and all He asked in return was for us to believe?"

The authority with which I had delivered these words had surprised me. As did Clara's reaction.

"But what has He actually given to me, Edward?" she snapped in, "God, knows I've waited. If He is actually there, why has He never done anything for me?"

She kicked over the remaining pieces on the board and seemed to turn away. But almost in the same movement she returned to face me, and without warning, for the first and only time, she kissed me.

Our debate had felt important, but there seemed to be so many more questions - so much left unresolved. I had wanted to add, that the very fact we were having this conversation — that we had somehow found each other to discuss this — was perhaps another reason to believe. But before I got the chance, she had stood up and walked away.

David and Sam had found my relationship with Clara intriguing at the start, but for different reasons had become less enthusiastic and wearier of it as the week progressed. For Sam, the thrill of my having gained access to her precious world quickly passed, and once he sensed things were stalling between us, he eventually got bored of asking for updates. David came to understand that more significant forces were enacting upon us. He recognized that my own growth in God during the week was steadily pulling me in a different direction than she would have me go.

As usual, he was right. I did not exactly perceive Clara as an enemy to Christianity, but if our conversation on the chess board had shown me anything, it was that she viewed it as something that could be defeated with logic. Whereas, I respected her views and even admired the vigor with which she defended them, for her, things were more black and white. If God had failed to deliver her miracle then it was inconceivable that anyone else could really be experiencing their's.

Clara's strange resolve to push me into choosing between our friendship and my own budding Christian beliefs came to a head on the penultimate afternoon of the holiday. She had arrived at my room - even though this was strictly forbidden by the Hathernwray rules - and lay petulantly on my bed, knowing that even though I was uneasy at her being there, I was too polite to ask her to leave.

"I'm leaving tonight. I'm leaving this place and all its loonies."

"To go where?" I responded, half suspecting that this was a fanciful plan she had spontaneously created in order to provoke a reaction.

"Anywhere, but home. Come with me?"

True or not, her proposal made me feel awkward and inevitably led to me disappointing her in a way that was typical of our time together. The implications of running away like that were far reaching, but above all else, I felt like there was more I needed to absorb from Hathernwray before I was ready to leave. God was speaking to me, calling me, challenging me more every hour - and not even Clara could make me cut this short.

Nonetheless, that night I lay awake in bed, thinking about her and fearing that she might actually go. I had earlier confided in my roommates to tell them what she had said, but as her words now replayed in my mind, my own sense of responsibility for the situation nagged away at me and made me restless.

The probability that Clara *had* been sincere seemed to increase dramatically when she wasn't there at breakfast in the normal way the next morning. My head began to race with questions about where she might be and what might happen next. I would inevitably be asked what I knew of her disappearance and each answer I rehearsed in my head seemed to make me sound more irresponsible for letting her leave alone. Most of all, I wondered whether she was safe and I rebuked myself for not having taken her more seriously. If I had, I would have surely tried harder to talk her out of it.

I was delighted then, when I saw Clara across the other side of the hall as we gathered for morning worship. We were seated several rows apart, so I was unable to catch her glance either before or during the meeting, but set off to her side of the room the moment it ended. My quest to congratulate her on the decision she had come to was, however, unexpectedly intercepted.

"I want to see you in the office," came an authoritative and familiar voice. It was Reverend Richard Stipe, one of the Hathernwray Hall leaders.

Although acutely surprised, I desperately tried to buy myself some time, "but, I've just got to..."

"Now!" His normally cordial tone temporary became more strained, and I instinctively knew not to argue.

Clara had tried to leave. Fortunately *they* had been tipped off, and clearly aware of their duty of care towards their residents, had quickly got to work trying to anticipate her likely movements. She had gotten no further than the nearby Cheltenham train station, before she was picked up.

My own confusion as to why I had been summoned there disappeared when I was told that she had been discovered with a train ticket to Coventry – *my* return ticket home. It immediately dawned on me that it had been taken from my room the previous afternoon and now she had implicated me in her plan by suggesting that I had willingly given this up to facilitate the first leg of her journey.

"Is this correct Edward? Because if not – if the ticket was taken from you - well then this becomes even more serious. We operate a policy of trust between residents and there are certain things we cannot tolerate."

Of course, I couldn't bring myself to land Clara in more trouble, and though untrue, I reluctantly confirmed my own role in her foiled getaway.

Given the circumstances, the normal practice would have been to send Clara straight home, but two things probably prevented this. Firstly, we were all due to leave the following morning anyway, and the effort required to reorganize her travel arrangements just to cut short the holiday by a few hours would have made this slightly farcical. Secondly, this punishment would have also have meant her traveling alone, which given the circumstances of the previous evening seemed an inappropriate risk in every respect.

I was similarly left in no doubt that my own behavior in this unfortunate episode was unacceptable. Reverend Stipe firmly conveyed that should I apply to attend Hathernwray Hall again, it was highly questionable whether I would be accepted to return. At this time and given the significance of the last few days, it was a penalty that left me winded with sadness.

Clara, had somehow led me to lie for her - led me to sin. I was not sure whether she took any particular satisfaction in this latest demonstration of her power, and I did not want to find out. I spent the rest of the day tucked away in the conservatory towards the rear of the estate; a place I had barely spent any time in before and certainly never gone to with her. Here, I numbly listened to the most morose songs I could find to play through my stereo's headphones, and watched the grey sky tip its contents rhythmically against the window.

At certain times in my life, the pace of things have seemed too quick for the head and heart to keep up. Its as if people or events reach into your consciousness just long enough to affect the way you feel, but pass away before you get the chance to really know or understand them. In the same way, everything that had happened at Hathernwray Hall, had now left me feeling slightly breathless, giddy and disoriented. I was tired but restless at the same time. Homesickness had begun to creep up on me.

By early evening, some of my disappointment had played out and I was grateful to hear the familiar and chirpy voices of David and Sam, who had come to collect me on the way to the evening worship meeting.

"Here you are. Seriously mate, I know it's hard, but if you can just keep up the pretense of wanting to hang around with us for a little while longer, you can go home tomorrow," the latter joked.

One conclusion I had come to during the day, was that David was probably the one who told the Hathernwray leaders about Clara's plans the previous evening. There was the potential for him to feel slightly uneasy about this, despite the fact I was actually very grateful to him for it, so I gave him a warm pat on the back to reassure him that he need not be concerned.

We were in the hall for a few minutes before I noticed Clara walk timidly down the aisle towards the left of our seats. While I tried not to watch her too attentively as she made her way past, my curiosity must have overcome me, given that in this time I saw her look towards me, bow her head, and then look up again before finding her seat. On the second occasion, she mouthed the words 'I'm so sorry,' before offering a modest, apologetic smile. I somehow managed not to respond.

The worship meeting itself was truly thrilling – life changing. I remember thinking that words spoken in prayer were *so* doused in truth and love that they must surely be more significant than what they meant in that time and place – somehow fundamental and timeless for our entire race. The hymns seemed to transmit a blessing that touched people both collectively and personally at the same time. I sang the words of Graham Kendrick's hymn, *Shine Jesus Shine*, like they might be the last ever to fall from my lips.

I cannot believe that anyone there could have been in any doubt, that heavenly powers were at work in the room. Our hearts thumped and eyes welled as, wave upon wave, a realization that God was with us took hold.

The culmination of this was when the residents were given the chance to make their own testimony of faith to the rest of the group. One after another they walked up to the front, and in a way that was enriched by the raw and unprepared manner of their delivery, they shared experiences and beliefs that moved us all profoundly.

Remarkably – inexplicably – I became one of them.

Normally talking to such a large number of people would be something I simply wouldn't contemplate; the thought of public speaking typically made me sick with nerves, especially during those years when teenage self-consciousness affected me the most. But on this occasion, when I stared out at the room of expectant faces, none of that mattered. I stood there almost without fear, and willingly told them *my* story – a story that both before and after seemed the most private thing conceivable.

My words were probably simple and ineloquent, but the truth is that I cannot recollect the exact content or language of what I shared. I simply remember stating what I had come to believe during the past six days - that God had entered my life in a 'big' way. It was the difference between accepting His existence and that He has a role to play in your life - and knowing that He must become *the* purpose of your life.

I felt ready to continue my journey. In many ways, I felt ready to leave.

Edward's Choice

I had caught sight of Clara at the back of the room while I was talking. Although even she could not have interrupted my focus during those amazing moments, I did notice that she had sobbed frantically through it all.

Afterwards, she approached me; her still reddened and slightly swollen face betraying the fact that she too had been moved by the last few hours.

She made what was to be her final demand of me, "come for a walk with me – I need you."

I wanted to help Clara. I wanted to know why she had cried and to find out whether the things she heard that evening had changed the way she felt about God. But right now, this was *my* time.

"Clara I'm sorry, but I'm going swimming." And with that, I turned my back on her and began walking back up the path towards the dormitories where the others were waiting.

Maybe, I was wrong. Perhaps not being there to guide Clara in what could have been her moment of discovery was the wrong thing to do. But whenever I've looked back on that decision, it has never been with the sense that I had refuted God's asking.

Certainly, later that night, as I lay on my inflatable ring, it felt wholly the right thing to have done. Just for those few seconds, and for the first time, I knew I had invested everything in Him and experienced the most magnificent sense of weightlessness. My life was suspended in faith and trust. I was in His hands and I knew I was a Christian.

Although very young, I look back upon that week and that night, as the platform for my Christian life since. Much of what I have come to hold as true and important in terms of how I have judged my own life, emanated from the beliefs and hopes that were formed during those days.

Back at home, many of the group that were experimentally thrown together during the holiday soon became a Christian youth group based from my parents' local church just as they had envisaged. And for a period, it would go on to fulfill some of this vast promise, serving an important role in the next stage of our Christian lives.

I have never returned to Hathernwray Hall in the time since, but have always hoped – liked to think - that it is still the way I remember it: a service-station on the way to heaven, where young Christians pick up directions, or else fill up on faith before dipping back onto the dusty road they call life.

I knew even then, that things would be different at home; that I would have to move on, and it was what I would take back that really mattered, rather than the place itself. I simply hoped that Clara also realized that she had a part to play in finding her miracle, and wouldn't simply go on waiting for it to happen. I certainly felt like God was calling me – inviting me into my Christian life. There would be other blessings to receive and other trials to face.

Secret Agent

Every summer seems to change you deeply when you are young. Like tides moving in and out of your life, some of the beliefs you once held firm are washed away, while the footprints and signatures of new people and what they have meant, are left with you.

The trouble I've had is that I've always been easily affected. Perhaps because of an instinctive sense that everything happens for a reason, I haven't always been able to discern between moments that would change me irreversibly, and feelings that would prove less permanent.

On reflection, I've had a tendency to overestimate the relevance of things. While I was never the sort of kid to buy into every fleeting teenage fad, fashion, or pop group, I would argue with anyone that the music I *did* like was revolutionary. Similarly, the groups of friends I've had at various times were characterised by attitudes that seemed so important and real, that I felt I was at the centre of some movement or sub-culture that would change the world.

It is only years later I have been able to look back and reflect upon the occasions when I was misguided, as well as see where my landscape had actually changed.

A few weeks break from school can seem like much longer. Each year, every kid but yourself seems to return looking so much older and more self-assured then what they had been just six weeks before. Even returning for the final year of my compulsory education, the sense of nervousness at re-joining this unpredictable and complicated society was the same.

The week at Hathernwray Hall *had* changed my life, but it was amazing how on the eve of the first day, it was the values and judgements that everybody else would bring back that dominated my mind, rather than how Christianity had changed me. My triumphant cry to the world about my commitment to God had become a scared whimper. I wanted to fit in again.

The feeling of fearful apprehension stirred me from my sleep several times through the night, and followed me to school on that first day. As I stepped out of the front door, my mind had already begun to fill with questions: What would life be like back at school? - Would I somehow seem different now that I was a Christian? - What if someone actually knew about Hathernwray or the church youth group I had started to attend?

But I had some time before I needed to find the answers. My journey would ordinarily take around half an hour at the dawdling pace I chose to adopt. I decided that the first part - from my house to the edge of the estate by the park — was my time. This section of my route, for roughly fifteen minutes, was used for prayer or to daydream about being back at Hathernwray. Here, I felt I could still be the *real* Edward.

After that, as I steadily approached school, I would start to address those difficult questions, and almost unconsciously, rehearse the person I would be when entering the school gates.

Just weeks after dedicating my life completely to Him, I was already trading portions of my time with the world. It was a process and timetable that I would follow on the same journey almost every day for the rest of the school year.

I have no reason to believe that my school was anything other than typical of other state schools on the first day back after the summer holidays. And like other institutions, the scene found within our fifth grade social room was a fascinating window on teenage life: young people frantically trying to establish their position on the pyramid of popularity, or in other cases, demonstrate their defiance.

Those at the top of the system dominated the room. Generally dressed in trendy variations of the school uniform, they sat in the pivotal seats around the stereo, clearly enjoying their status. Tough kids – with huge muscular frames and facial hair that seemed impossible for their age – eyed the more popular children with threatening disdain. And then there were the kids who, entirely intentionally, were less mainstream and slightly weird in appearance. Ignoring the music from the main stereo, and seemingly oblivious to everyone else, they instead bobbed up and down like cogs within a machine to the indie or rock beats and guitars that played from their own headphones. Intermingled with them were sporty kids, funny kids, gossiping kids, kids with their heads already in books.

But what sort of kid was I? Had I without realizing it, become the 'religious' kid over the summer? I suddenly became concerned that my Christianity might somehow be apparent – like it was written across my forehead and it was just a matter of time before people began to notice.

But right now no one noticed me, and the growing and uncomfortable sense of my own insignificance, even invisibility, did not feel good either.

I was released from my watching brief by a tap on my shoulder.

"And how did the summer treat you, Eddy-boy?" spoke a confident and rhythmic voice.

Jared was someone I had steadily become acquainted with the year before. Having bumped into him in town one Saturday and shared the bus ride home, we had discovered a mutual fondness for certain films, and following that he had made an effort to talk to me whenever our paths crossed.

"Yeah...it was good," I said, trying hard not to think about Hathernwray.

Jared was definitely someone who was less easy to categorise, but if one group could own him, it would be the 'popular' crowd. He had long thick black hair

Jonathan Young

and deep-set intriguing eyes that contributed to his sense of importance and intensity. He was wearing a dark robe-like cardigan above a slightly creased looking school shirt that was typical of his dress sense.

He was a fascinating character and for many he performed the unsolicited role of forecaster, leader, and general authority for all things 'cool.' He would often be the one to break a new band or introduce a different way of dressing to the rest of the year group. Moreover, the way he spoke was intriguing – always with a tempo and tone that made it almost poetic.

He went on to fill me in on the details of his summer break: what seemed an incredible experience working in a theatre, where, as well as spending time with some extraordinary characters, he attended almost every backstage party that was thrown.

Where I was anxious and uncomfortable about being back, he seemed to thrive on the uncertainty of it all and was completely at ease with the situation. Now and then he interrupted himself to pass comment on other pupils who had returned looking somehow different, or to nod in the direction of another friend.

Despite my own reservations, the conversation with Jared had the effect of easing me back into the school environment. As we scuttled off to register, I suddenly felt more equipped to deal with things, especially as everyone must by now have noticed him enthusiastically talking to me.

As with other years, my thoughts of what the first school day would be like proved to be somewhat pessimistic. I was a reasonably likeable kid and had no real reason to be fearful of this environment, even if I had purposely stayed around the fringes of things previously. Almost before I knew it one lesson seemed to merge into the next, and one day into the one after that, until the first week was over. I slowly allowed myself to think that things could just be okay.

The church youth group had a successful first few weeks, carried in part, by the momentum of the Hathernwray Hall holiday. For those of us that had been there, the idea of somehow re-creating the enjoyment and 'spirit' of our week away for an hour or so each week was very appealing.

We would meet every Sunday after the main church evening worship, and during that time have discussions around certain passages in the Bible, sing hymns, and in the early days, talk about Hathernwray — a lot. It was a fillip that for the first few weeks of school, I felt I could hardly do without.

But of course, the group wasn't ours to selfishly guard. We just happened to be there at the beginning. Word got around about what we were doing and almost every week more people joined us. At the start, they were friends or brothers and sisters of the initial members, but very soon there were teenagers turning up from other churches that were further away. The age range of the attendees expanded as well. There were suddenly different sub-groups of friends, and with them, varying expectations of the weekly meeting.

Whether we liked it or not — and most of the original group didn't initially — our purpose would have to change and to grow. To truly be a vehicle for God's work we would have to finally move on from the summer and look to the future, and the leaders realized this.

Jared and I became good friends. Perhaps because I was a familiar face in the set he had been put in for the majority of subjects that year, or because he felt inclined to adopt me as his project for the same vague reasons or qualities that Clara had, we spent an increasing amount of time together.

Whatever the reason, Jared also worked like an agent on my behalf to the other kids. Whereas the majority of the people who 'counted' within my year group were perhaps initially sceptical of me - unconvinced about my credentials to hang around based on previous years — it was clear from a steady change in attitude towards me that he was actively promoting my case.

This was done subtly, of course, but he also realized that most people at that age dealt in superficial headlines rather than detail. Accordingly, he would

Jonathan Young

simply feed them positive references to me like, 'He's a good bloke,' or 'top fella,' whenever I cropped up in conversation. For the occasions he did feel some more background information would be useful, I came to realize that he would embellish things I had told him, or in some cases, even make things up completely to give his case the edge.

One such occasion was when he told another pupil that I had a regular DJ slot at a youth club Disco out of town. Having overheard this, and aware that I had not said anything that could make him believe it, I reluctantly decided to raise the issue.

"I know you're only trying to help mate," I said apprehensively, "but you know that's not true, don't you?"

"Don't worry about it Eddie-boy. And don't worry about those chimps," he said disparagingly. "In a few days they won't remember anyway. They'll only care that it's okay to like you because their chimp best mate likes you."

His lips were pursed in an assured, knowing smile. I immediately felt absurd for even mentioning it to him.

Steadily he propelled me to another level; one that made school a great deal easier than I had experienced before. The thought of life outside was still an important release, but the idea of thriving and becoming someone within the school-gates slowly became attractive as well.

Occasionally, I even stopped over at Jared's house after we had been to house parties together or spent the night watching films. During those evenings, we would sometimes slope off to a small area of woodland behind his house so that we could smoke cigarettes and drink vodka from a small hip flask he would carry. I did not particularly enjoy either at that stage, but it was then that Jared was at his best - talking insightfully about people we knew, sharing bizarre stories from his life, making me laugh, and most of all, making me feel like his best friend.

I sensed things were changing, but tried hard not to give any consideration to whether this was for the better or worse. I had obviously seen friends outside of school before, but now more than ever my aspirations seemed more geared towards this part of my life.

Having noted my own ascent up the teenage pecking order, my mistake was to begin viewing all the other pupils as part of the same crude league table. And for some reason my attitude to those I perceived as ranked much lower than myself, became more haughty and belittling with each passing day.

Someone I unfairly viewed in such terms was a boy called Shaun Rainsforth. He had moved to the area from Rochdale around a month into the school term, which seemed strange for such a pivotal examination year. Clearly without friends to call on from previous terms, and having started even this one late, it was as if he was playing catch-up thereafter in every sense.

Shaun was slim and scruffy looking, with fair untrained hair that rose from his head in all different directions. He was reasonably tall, but seemed to walk around with his head apologetically bowed, and frequently dipped his face into a grimy looking handkerchief to blow his nose or clean his spectacles. There were initially rumours that he had been excluded from his previous school, but having seen the unobtrusive way he went about his business here, it was difficult to imagine him doing anything conspicuous enough to warrant such consequences.

Unfortunately, Shaun's struggle to impose his personality on the school in any meaningful way, coupled with his new boy 'status,' made him an easy target for the shallow mockery of other pupils in the first few weeks.

The tone for the teasing he received was cruelly set during his first day in class. As was fairly typical in these circumstances, he had been asked by our class tutor, Mr. Podolski, to stand and introduce himself, but such was his anxiety, even this was made to seem like an unreasonable request.

Clearly fraught with nerves, for a few seconds he had fidgeted between a seated and upright position – bobbing his head up and down as if he might already be dodging some sort of ammunition from his classmates. When he eventually did find his feet, his attempt to complete what he'd started became even more painful to behold.

"My name's, Sh...Sh..." He initially crocked out, before allowing his voice to give way to a large intake of breath.

"My name's Sh..."

Again, he couldn't finish.

The colour had drained from his face as silence temporarily suffocated the room. But for a final time, he filled his lungs, seemingly determined to bring this terror to an end himself, before Mr. Podolski might step in to rescue him.

"My name is Sh...Shaun Rainsforth, Sir."

And with that, he dropped to his seat.

It was only a stutter, but thereafter he hardly stood a chance. Even moments later, a boy callously whispered, "Sh...Sh...Shaun," from the back of the room. The taunt would be repeated for weeks, almost routinely whenever he was around.

There were those who felt sorry for Shaun, but only occasionally did they find the courage to defend him against his tormentors.

I found myself equally reticent to stick my head out on his behalf. I had other things to worry about, and despite a slight sense of guilt about my inaction from time to time, I knew I would quickly kick-off that uneasy feeling.

Besides, what could I really do? It was impossible to fight the cause of every kid that was bullied at school, and at that stage Shaun *was* just another kid.

The church youth leaders set about promoting a new focus for the group by setting up a short biblical assignment, based on Jesus' disciples. Predictably, we were split into groups of *their* choosing in order to do this, to encourage the integration of the newer members.

With each group having been allocated a disciple for the exercise, the idea was for us to depict their experiences from the time leading up to Jesus' crucifixion, until the point He rose from the dead. How we did this was up to us — a diary, picture board, or song — but we were specifically asked to try and represent how they might have felt on a personal level through that period, as well as what we are told about them in the New Testament. We would get together for an hour or so to work on this the following week, before sharing our work with the others during the main youth group meeting.

I was aware that Judas was a bad pick, but was neither pleased nor disappointed when Simon Peter was chosen for my group as the subject for our task. I was also aware that David and I had been placed in a group with three kids who were a year or so younger than us. One of them, a girl called Sally, volunteered her house as a meeting place to discuss what we would do.

What I couldn't have known, as I knocked on Sally's door that next Sunday, was that our group had been joined by a new member. Sally's mom told me that the others had already arrived as she enthusiastically escorted me towards where they had gathered, while at the same time asking me if I wanted a drink. As I approached the room, I could hear several voices that I recognized, but one of these stood-out as being unexpected. Like when you turn on the radio and hear someone being interviewed that you know you are familiar with, but can't quite place, this was someone I knew, but somehow out of context.

Sally's mom courteously knocked and pushed the door open, prompting me to enter. I eagerly looked in to identify the voice's owner, and when I did, could not quite believe who my eyes fixed upon. There at the other end of the room was Shaun Rainsforth; chatting to the others, smiling and then looking up at me.

"Here they are," said Sally's mom warmly. "I think you might have already met Shaun at school? He lives 'round the corner and is going to start coming to the group. Isn't that great? Did you say lemonade would be okay?"

I nodded numbly to all three questions, before coldly and timidly nodding again towards Shaun to acknowledge him. I suddenly felt ill at ease; like an intruder had broken into my bedroom and was threatening to sift through my

Jonathan Young

most private possessions.

Immediately, the implications of his arrival at the group began to explode into my mind in a way I found impossible to process. I have the type of brain that prefers time to work through things slowly, but here I felt like I had been rushed into the operating theatre with my inner-voice screaming at me to stop the bleeding of one side of my life into the other. I couldn't quite get my head around it. I just knew it was bad – very bad.

Although I seemed to get lost in my own thoughts, the rest of the team worked eagerly together on the task we had been given. It had struck me as a strange brief at first, but looking back, the leaders were probably aware of the difficulties the group faced in taking their Christian beliefs from the church youth group environment into their daily lives. I suspect they were hoping we could draw strength from realizing that even the disciples would have experienced a sense of solitude, doubt, and fear when they were apparently left alone in the world, only to rediscover a stirring to take forward Jesus' message when He came to them again.

Focusing upon Peter certainly ensured that this was the essence of what was discussed within our group, and what we later shared with the others. This was done through a series of cartoon-type drawings on large sheets of paper with us each taking it in turns to describe, or in some cases, act out each of the scenes. David contributed his usual intelligence and wit to the proceedings, responding to the accusation that his speech betrayed him as a follower of Jesus, by humorously exaggerating his west midlands accent when denying Him for the final time.

For Shaun's part, he was more vocal and confident than I had ever seen him at school. He contributed in a way that made the others slowly warm to him. David even made a point of telling me he thought he was 'alright' at the end of the evening, which summed up his modest but positive impact.

Deep down, I probably shared this assessment – Shaun *was* alright – but whatever I thought of him, he had given me a problem to deal with. How would

I react to him at school? How would the others respond to the fact I even knew him in this context? There was a chance that people would actually find out about the youth group.

It would be a busy fifteen minutes from the park to school the following morning.

I had not set out with the intention of being secretive about the church youth group - it had just happened. I seemed to stiffen with fear whenever there was even a chance that this part of my life would become unveiled, from the infrequent occasions the conversation would turn to 'God' or religion, to times I might simply be asked what I had done the previous Sunday.

I could not overcome a growing sense that these were two hopelessly incompatible worlds.

You see, however much you believe that Christianity permeates the beliefs and values of society, you have to accept that things are slightly different through a schoolchild's eyes. The idea that Christianity provides a comfortable backdrop to education — an implicit part of what is learned and reinforced - is difficult to swallow for the kid who cries all the way home because they have been called a 'bible-basher' in class.

Certainly for me, the fact that religious tendencies of any kind could be mercilessly mocked at school was an uneasy truth I almost wanted to protect my parents from knowing. For the pupils who decided to let on to their beliefs, whatever they happened to be, the best they could hope for was to be judged as weird or horridly old-fashioned.

For that reason, the thought of declaring my own faith was wholly unappealing. Besides, Jared had worked so hard on my credibility, and suddenly undermining this would feel like I was also throwing everything he had done for me back in his face.

At least, this was how I somewhat superficially chose to view the situation.

Jonathan Young

Thinking about it now, Jared was perhaps the one person who might have found it interesting - even fun - especially if this made me peculiar and different to the majority of the year group. I never really dared to ask him.

Instead, I busied myself trying to avoid the scenario whereby Shaun might try to discuss the church youth group in front of Jared. I watched them both intensely whenever they happened to be in the same room, and manufactured reasons to drag Jared away if they got too close. It was like directing a particularly difficult scene in a play, where neither of the main characters had been allowed to see the script.

I made it through to Friday before my secret was genuinely threatened. But then as Jared and I were walking out of the school gates at lunchtime, I saw Shaun approaching from the opposite direction.

Almost instinctively I quickened my stride, hoping we could ghost past without him noticing, and was initially relieved when I spotted that his eyes arrowed downwards in the usual fashion, as if he might be counting his own footsteps. Having marched on for several strides, I allowed myself to believe we had passed undetected.

But that same moment, Shaun's voice rose above the schoolyard din, as if to tap me on the shoulder.

"See you on Sunday?"

I am ashamed to admit that my instinct was to continue walking at this point, hurtfully and cowardly pretending not to have heard the question. Unfortunately, Jared had no reason to behave so ridiculously, and having also heard, he casually turned around to face Shaun, leaving me no option but to do likewise.

"See you on Sunday?" Shaun repeated, this time with more emphasis.

"Sunday? yeah right. Erm, *Sunday*." I absurdly revisited the word, as if it represented some sort of riddle that I had to quickly decipher.

Suddenly, I was the one struggling to find any meaningful words to say. I looked at Shaun and then up at Jared, almost wanting to apologise for dragging him into this embarrassing situation. Despite the number of times I had practiced what I might say to divert or hijack *this* conversation when it occurred, I knew I was making a mess of things.

I am not sure how long the ensuing pause lasted, but it was enough for the awkwardness to infect all three of us. It took Jared to break the stalemate.

"Listen mate, catch me up, yeah?"

He stared at me for a couple of seconds before turning to walk away. And in that stare I detected disappointment – perhaps even irritation – as well as an understandable confusion about what exactly was happening. It was a look that seemed to say 'listen mate, I'm not sure what all this is about, but stop being such a fool about it.'

With that I turned around to Shaun. By now I was feeling increasingly humiliated and annoyed, and unfairly took this out on him with the curt tone of my reply.

"Yeah, okay I'll see you Sunday. Just one thing - you're a decent bloke, but things are different here at school. I've got my mates already and..."

"Right, different." He cut me off before my sentence became any more wounding.

Shaun breathed a sigh of resignation through his nostrils and his eyes moved wildly to reveal real anger at how pathetically I was behaving. And with that he walked off, without saying anything else.

I was never faced with having to explain the uncomfortable encounter with Shaun at the school gates, as Jared didn't raise the subject again. But that did not stop me replaying the whole situation over and over in my head that evening. Ironically, as I did this, I found that I cared less about what Jared may have thought and more about the despicable way I had behaved towards Shaun.

I made up my mind to try and straighten things out with him during the church youth group, and was pleased that I would only have to wait a day or so before I had my opportunity.

Jonathan Young

It was not that I particularly had anything more positive to say to Shaun. My predicament regarding him remained the same and the idea of us being friends at school still seemed impossible. But like when you have to call a relative to apologise for forgetting their birthday, I hoped he could at least respect me for facing up to him, even if I could not really alter what had passed.

I was therefore pleased to see him already waiting on the railings beside the door to the church vestry where the group was held, when I was dropped off that Sunday. Even though this conversation had the potential to be every bit as difficult as the one which had made it necessary, I stepped out of the car with real purpose and began to walk towards him.

Unfortunately, I would be diverted from my task almost immediately. My attention was drawn away from Shaun to where the silhouettes of three figures noisily approached from further up the road. The sound of their voices barking conversation too and fro echoed around the street and filled my stomach with a churning anxiety. The thing was, I realized straight-away that these were voices from school - these were boys from my year-group.

Knowing that I hadn't been spotted by either them or Shaun at this stage, I instinctively stepped sideways into the shadows of the main church building where I could not be seen. Again, I felt compelled to guard my association with the group like a shameful secret.

Shaun had no such inclination, and no hiding place. And *they* were the sort of characters to make him pay.

"Look here lads, its Sh…Sh…Shaun, and he's going to church," goaded one of them.

"Sunday-school finished hours ago, Rainsforth — what are you doing?" said one of the others, before heaving out a laugh that seemed shallow and gratuitous.

"So this is where your friends are Rainsforth," continued another.

I suddenly felt angry at them, but mainly at myself. I closed my eyes and for a few seconds clasped my hands around my ears, nodding my head dementedly. I hated myself for lacking the courage to help Shaun and could not stand to listen to his ordeal anymore.

Then I asked God to make it stop.

I opened and re-focused my eyes just in time to see Shaun disappear into the vestry doors with the arm of one of the group leaders draped protectively around his shoulder. At the other side of the street, the boys scurried up an ally-way, as if the light that temporarily shined from within had made the evil retreat. To my great relief, he was safe.

But I had lost my chance, and for that evening at least, I'd also lost my motivation and courage to speak to him.

Although, I never told my parents, I didn't go to the church youth group at all that night. Instead I walked home by myself, trying to remember exactly who I was.

Without really speaking, Shaun and I seemed to arrive at a temporary agreement as to how we would act towards each other. None of this was his fault, but he probably felt some responsibility for coming between me and the church youth group, and would have known from the others there just how important it was to me. Therefore, while he clearly wouldn't go out of his way to repair the situation between us, he would not intentionally make my life any more difficult either – and for the time-being that meant giving me some breathing-space.

As for how I had behaved towards him, I was still unsure of how I could make things better but kidded myself that I would be there for him the next time he really needed my support. Though I had refused to feel responsible for him when he first turned-up, somehow a sense of obligation had now developed through everything that had happened.

I would of course, fail him for a final time. Things came to a head again about two weeks later, during a lesson on 'Social and Environmental Studies'

- a period on our timetable that most students regarded as a break from 'more serious' subjects. The class wasn't tied to any formal qualification, but for those who turned up – and many didn't – it did offer a fairly diverse content, ranging from the learning of various life skills such as writing letters of application, to the opportunity to debate different social and moral issues.

The topic for discussion on the day in question was actually life-after-death. Jared in particular seemed fascinated by the debate, and eagerly listened to contributions both supporting and contesting the idea of an after-life. His enthusiasm was partly fuelled by a film he had recently watched which depicted the real life accounts of people involved in near-death experiences; all of whom claimed to have had glimpses of the 'other-side' in one form or other.

Inevitably, the conversation moved on from the consideration of whether there might be some sort of reality after death, to what or whom this might be. It was then that Mr. Podolski, who taught this lesson, shocked me – and probably the rest of my classmates - with a very direct question:

"Who actually believes in a god? Put your hands-up."

For some reason, I felt what he had asked was somehow off-limits – a corner in people's lives that he surely wasn't permitted to delve into.

In the event, it again had the effect of exposing my own lack of courage in standing up for my beliefs, and thankfully, of reconfirming Shaun's strength. His was one of only three or so hands that bravely reached into the air.

Mine remained pitifully rooted beneath the table. I wanted to be counted among the *believers* – I wanted to put my hand up – but felt I needed to assess the reaction to those that had first. I just needed a few more seconds to see how things would develop.

Mr. Podolski surveyed the room to assess the results of his spontaneous poll, and even looked like he might go one step further to begin asking people to explain their views. But before he got this opportunity, one of the boys that had turned up outside the church on that Sunday a fortnight or so before, decided it was down to him to depict Shaun's Christian life.

"Shaun's a proper member of the God Squad sir, we saw him down there the other night. We reckon he's one of those happy-clapper worshipers – I bet he's got a tambourine and everything."

Laughter broke out. Shaun seemed to look towards Mr. Podolski to rescue him from the crisis he had inadvertently caused. And yet, with his hand still raised, *he* was the next person to speak.

"Yeah I go to church. And yeah I believe in God – so what?"

This reignited the laughter, but Shaun had not finished. He seemed to be growing in strength.

"So what if I do?" he continued, "you lot seem pretty curious? At least curious enough to hang around and watch me go in. Maybe you want to find out about God as well? Or is it just that you've got nothing better to do?"

"Watch your mouth Rainsforth," the boy retorted angrily. "I wouldn't want to hang around with your types. The further you and your religious freaks stay away from me the better."

The next thing to happen, changed the atmosphere in the room to such a degree, that it seemed God Himself had sucked away the oxygen to silence Shaun's oppressor. In fact, it was Jared who entered the argument.

"And what exactly do *you* believe?" he said, looking at the boy, "...if there isn't a god waiting for us after we die, what's your theory about all this?"

The look on both his face and that of Shaun's summed up the surprise that was felt by everyone in the room. Where there was commotion and raucousness before, his challenge was greeted with surprise and a deathly silence.

"No, I thought so, you haven't got one. So how about you give him a break?" he continued, having allowed his now defeated opponent to feel the stinging discomfort of his speechlessness for a few seconds.

And with that, as if the debate had tipped decisively to one side, Jared too raised his hand.

"You know what, I think *he's* probably right - there is a god up there," he concluded.

Maybe he suddenly believed, maybe he didn't, but for that moment he was in union with Shaun. The momentum was now with them, and I finally felt confident enough to join them. I was ready to show my faith. Now I was ready.

Without warning, the rest of the class sprang to their feet; like the coil that had been tightening through the tense final exchanges, had suddenly released, thrusting them out of their chairs.

Only I remained seated. I had been so engrossed by what had passed that I had somehow failed to even notice the bell ringing to signal the end of the school day. My declaration would not be made and my sense of failure was compounded.

A moment later, I thought I might have heard a rooster crow. As I turned to walk out of school, my head filled with thoughts of Peter and tears were in my eyes.

There have been times when I've misjudged the impact people are making upon me; typically overrating the extent to which their lives might leave an imprint on my own. But that term, in different ways, the steely conviction of Shaun and Jared - the way they both created their reality in a way that wasn't propped up by the world — would leave an impression upon me that has remained ever since.

Shaun in particular, had the power to make me examine myself like few other people. He was strong where I was weak. He had courage where I had fear. We shared a great truth, but his actions did so much more to make this apparent than my own.

As for Jared, I had perhaps believed that he was at the very source of those forces which had distracted me from my faith in the last few weeks. But looking back, in reality those forces came from within me.

I would come to understand that the sense of school-yard prestige that I discovered during that period, and which had become so precious to me, would only wear me down. It would ultimately make me as inconsequential as a grain of sand dragged down the beach by the indiscriminate tide.

But that realization would not arrive with me yet. For now, the need to divorce the two parts of my life would go on. In fact I felt that, for the time being, this was the easiest way to be.

I was still committed to my Christian life; I just made up my mind that I could best serve Him in a more subtle way – undercover if you like. I'd be much better placed to do His work from the inside, where I could get close to people. I'd have more impact from there.

From now on, I decided I would not just be a soldier in God's holy army, I would be part of his secret service. I would change from being Edward the Christian - the teenager - the school kid, to being 'Edward – a secret agent for the God Squad.'

Choices

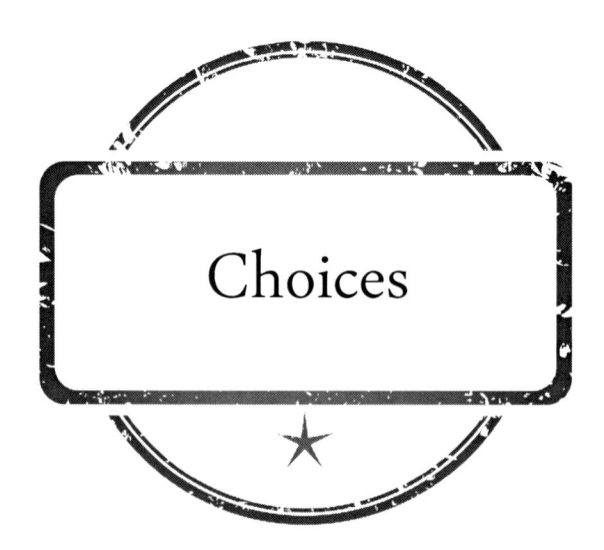

Christianity can seem like a calling to serve, but it can also seem like a safety net. You see, if you feel like you already know the end - if you believe you're saved, there's the temptation to retreat into an ordinary life - to amble along - to effectively wait for heaven.

The responsibility Jesus gave to His disciples was very different to this. They were asked to continue the work that God had sent His only Son to earth to begin. When you think about it, how could their mission have been any greater?

There were plenty of occasions when I had the option of choosing a different Christian life, and making things less complicated for myself. There were opportunities to 'out' myself and make clear I was working for Jesus. But like when you get into a stupid argument where you're not completely sure your point of view is correct, it can often seem easier to carry on adding more layers of complexity in the hope of reaching the stage whereby your case achieves some validity, rather than admit your mistake. For years I elected to continue in my policy of frequently concealing my faith, convincing myself that this would turn out to be the right thing.

Moving away to college in Bristol was therefore a minor crossroads in my life. In the rare moments I was honest with myself, I conceded that up to this point, this approach had not really served God in the way I had persuaded myself it could. *The night* at the leisure centre with the trendily dressed speaker just a few months before, had felt like a release after several years of wrestling with my own guilt, but as the days passed, the rousing sense of purpose that initially gripped me seemed to ebb away. Indeed, in some ways, the fact I now felt more assured of my place in heaven, made it easier to postpone and compartmentalise my Christianity.

But here was the chance of a fresh start. At Bristol I would find a new set of people, and the opportunity to be more honest about who I was, without first having to unpick the mesh of falsity and misapprehension that I had allowed to envelop me at home.

This wasn't a strategy I had consciously plotted in the weeks, or even days, leading up to leaving. It was more a case of it creeping into my head more subtly among a crowd of other thoughts whenever I began to contemplate college and what it might be like. Not surprisingly, it filled my mind again as I threw the last of my belongings into the boot of my mother's Fiesta on the morning I was due to leave.

I had been allowed to borrow her car to make the move down to the college's halls of residence. Of course, my parents would have much preferred to have taken me there themselves, but unfairly, I cringed at the thought of arriving there with them in tow. I imagined them making blunt attempts to introduce me to other students, or in their exuberance to help me get set up, making me look over-pampered and helpless; though in reality, they probably were not any more likely to embarrass me than anyone else's mom and dad.

Despite the selfishness of it, they seemed to vaguely understand where I was coming from, and reluctantly agreed to let me go it alone, with understanding that they would drop by more discreetly to visit and pick up the car the following weekend. My mother also gave me several large food parcels that she had packed up to see me through the first few days, which of course, I was extremely grateful for.

One of the things that stands out about that morning, was just how nervous I was. I remember trying hard to focus my full attention on each of my family members, as one by one, they hugged me and wished me well, but my thoughts were already racing ahead. Going there seemed like such a big thing to contend with, that it was as if dealing with all the emotion of the separation, was more than I could take. So, consciously or not, as I reversed out the drive, gently pressing the horn to signal my goodbye, my eyes avoided my mom as she stood waving – knowing that her eyes would be reddening, preparing to let go her tears. I must have seemed cold and preoccupied but it was the only way I believed I could cope.

This wasn't to say I *was* dispassionate about leaving. Just a few moments later, when the road where I had always lived fully disappeared from my rear view mirror, I'd finally allow one of my own tear-drops escape the seal I'd imposed. In fact, now I knew I was alone and that it wouldn't make leaving any harder, I was happy to try and grasp the significance of those moments – to invite sentimentality in.

I drove by the park where I used to walk to get to school and imagined myself ambling along, mentally readying myself for the day ahead. I even indulged myself by diverting to pass a few of the other places that I felt were defining of the previous years: my school – an old café on the edge of town where my friends and I used to hang around - even the church hall where the youth group was held.

In some ways it didn't add up to much, and at this point, I wasn't sure how much of this – my life to date - I really wanted to take with me. I was optimistic that better things lay ahead; that God was about to give me the key to my Garden of Eden.

It was about ten minutes later that I joined the motorway, and began fishing around in the glove box for any audio tapes I may have left in there. The journey had begun to lose the sense of poignancy I wanted it to have, and having picked out and rejected a few different options, I eventually pushed a *Depeche Mode* album on the stereo, hoping this might revive the mood I wanted.

Almost every other car I passed seemed to contain an apprehensive looking kid of about my age, with the soon-to-be contents of their student bedroom packed in every available space around them. The possibility that they might even be heading to the same college as me, shot uncomfortably across my mind, and instantly made me feel self-aware as if they were somehow able to read my stream of consciousness. Instinctively, I shuffled upright in my seat and adjusted my sunglasses in the mirror, as if they were my defence to this type of imposition.

Wherever they were heading, it was clear that their lives were about to change dramatically. The chances were that *they* would change significantly. I imagined them hurriedly rehearsing the persona they would present when they arrived at their various destinations.

I still had work to do. The question of how I could once again become someone who was more open about their Christianity, lingered in my mind like a piece of homework that I'd somehow been sent in advance to starting my new college, and had thus far failed to complete. I imagined various stilted first conversations with other students at the bar that evening, and among the painful small talk, somehow having to make even more awkward attempts to slip my faith into the conversation.

I just couldn't do it – not like that. It was tantamount to hawking my Christianity around like a door-to-door salesperson, and was unlikely to achieve anything other than ensuring my first few weeks on campus would be very lonely.

Personal Jesus played from the stereo, and recognizing the odd relevance of the song's title, a subtle smile cracked the troubled landscape of my face.

I found myself wondering, 'what would David (Stone) do?' It's a question that I've asked myself many times in difficult circumstances. He was the one friend who seemed, without exception, to be able to say and do the right thing regardless of the thorniness of the situation he faced.

David would also be leaving Coventry that weekend to go to university in Leeds and I met up with him and Sam for a farewell 'drink' just a few nights earlier. It was good to catch up and find out what was happening with them, but I had been surprised and disappointed when they told me that the church youth group seemed destined to finish, given that many of its members were now moving away, or for other reasons, just not turning up anymore.

Despite this, you got the sense that David, more than anyone, did not really need the group or anyone else to prop up his convictions, be it now at home or when he arrived in Leeds. He was so comfortable with what he believed that you just couldn't imagine him being troubled by how he might break his Christianity to a new set of people in the way I was. He wouldn't push it on anyone, but when *that* moment arose – perhaps when he joined the university's Christian society, or late one night when he and his new friends might stumble into a conversation around religion or theology - he would just be himself and be led by truth.

Like so often in my life, *my* challenge was putting this truth ahead of my increasingly overbearing desire to make the right impression - to fit in. And acknowledging this, again I began to feel my own weakness keenly.

It was then I decided to do what I perhaps should have done long before - seek my guidance through prayer. I turned down my music, gathered my thoughts, and began to speak to *Him*.

'Father-in-heaven – please hear my prayer...'

Even if my faith was becoming less apparent to the outside world at this time, privately I still spoke to God in one way or another most days. And on most of those occasions it still felt like I was tuned into heaven – like His energy was feeding back down the line into my life. But recently, and increasingly so, there were also prayers that seemed disjointed and forced. On these occasions it was as if I was merely performing a duty that was a condition of my Christian life, and speaking more in hope than belief that I was being heard.

Unfortunately, after just a few seconds, it was clear that *this* would not be a prayer of real connection. My concentration was spoiled by the restless instinct to again rehearse the scenes and conversations that lay ahead. Even the traffic, which now slowed to a standstill, seemed to suffocate my focus. I felt boxed-in and inhibited by the other cars, like their drivers were listening in and gate-crashing my dialogue with God. It didn't occur to me then that these difficulties were symptomatic of me allowing the outside world to affect my choices relating to Him. In the end I stopped, broke-off – believing that I'd pick up where I left off later in the journey.

I pulled into the service station. It was one of those September days where the chilly air seems to be serving notice on the long summer, and I zipped-up my jacket to just below my nose before walking in.

Having visited the toilets and taken a cursory glance around the shop, I decided to grab a drink from one of the restaurants, and sat down by the window as far away from the relative hustle and bustle of the busy food serving area as I could get.

Without a book or newspaper to read, the people wandering to and from the main building became my casual entertainment. I again instinctively looked out for other teenagers who I could imagine becoming part of my life when in Bristol. But rather than them, my eyes fixed upon a tall elderly gentlemen, who was tensely clasping the straps of a large red rucksack that he was wearing. He was standing around ten metres or so from the large revolving doors, and caught my attention because of the way he agitatedly walked one way, and then the other, before stopping to stare out at the mass of vehicles that stood before him in the car park.

He looked lost, worried, confused – even panicky, and I instantly felt concerned for him. But at the same time, I found his vulnerability perversely absorbing and felt compelled to go on watching.

Jonathan Young

I could not be sure what exactly he was looking for – but he released his grip on the bag just long enough to rub his nearly-bald head, as if he was trying to massage out the solution to his problem from somewhere within. When this did not arrive, his sense of crisis appeared to heighten - peaking with an inexplicable little hop that his legs almost involuntarily produced, followed by a short stumble which almost led to a collision with a young woman who was walking purposely out of the main entrance. He looked embarrassed, dismayed, and frightened at the same time. I fidgeted in my seat, temporarily believing I should help him.

And for the next few moments, I'm sorry to say, I went on thinking I should. I was annoyed – both at myself and also at everyone else there, who noticing what was happening, allowed him to struggle on. Thankfully it wasn't much more than a minute before someone did bring the whole thing to an end. He *was* rescued.

A lady of similar age, but barely half his size, appeared as if out of nowhere and offered him a reassuring smile that was an immediate antidote to his dismay. She was clearly pleased to see him, but stopped short of hugging him or doing anything overly demonstrative, as if to save him the discomfort of anymore unwanted attention. Instead, clasping his coat sleeve, she mouthed the words "c'mon you," before coaxing him in the direction of their car.

I clearly didn't know who she was or how they were connected (although I guess she was probably his wife) but at that moment he looked back at her like he was staring into the eyes of an angel. His drama was over, and his life, which I imagined to be a happy one, was now possibly even better than before. As uncomfortable and fleeting as those moments had actually been, they had served to remind him of what he had. For a few seconds I was elated.

And then I felt flat. I got back in the car and assessing my mother's road atlas, calculated that I probably had around an hour and a half left to drive. Looking at the hundreds of roads crisscrossing across the page, it now struck me how chaotic and crowded my journey had been – and could still be. But it was more than that. *I* felt weary and alone. Right now, even waiting for heaven seemed like a hardship. Without realizing it, I had begun resenting the fact I could not have it here on earth. Why must life be such a trial?

For the remainder of that journey, my mood was very different to how it had been at the beginning. The anxiety that had gripped me was replaced by a numbing resolve just to deal with the next few hours, while the sense of expectation I had set out with had given way to an instinctive need to consolidate and 'get through' it. As I re-joined the motorway for the last time, the task of revealing my Christianity now seemed immense.

Indeed, it seemed a bridge too far. I began hoping that this wasn't God's wish after-all, and that my difficulty in finding the strategy to begin, was His way of pointing this out. I knew that my memory of passages from the Bible couldn't be relied on, and I'd not really been along to church to hear many recently, but I began to hope there was something written in scripture that might somehow justify my secrecy.

After a few moments of deliberation and prompting, I was somewhat surprised when a vague recollection of some words in Matthew *did* yield from the depths of my sub consciousness. I recalled guidance to enter by the 'narrow gate' and to take the 'difficult' way 'which leads to life' (Matthew 7:13-14), which I quickly persuaded myself had to be relevant. Perhaps this meant taking a less obvious approach to Christianity – doing His work through less obvious means. My train of thought and hypothesis were still very sketchy, but I was immediately buoyed by this interpretation. Staying under cover fitted this belief, while you could argue that choosing to wear my faith more openly was incompatible with it. For now, this was justification enough. Besides I was running out of time – I was always running out of time. I had to decide who and what I was going to be.

Having read '*Bristol 6*' from the large blue sign at the side of the motorway, I indicated to leave at the next junction. I inhaled heavily through my nostrils, as if for some reason I might now have to hold my breath from here until I arrived at my destination. I was getting closer, and after just a couple of blocks, the line of buildings aligning each road seemed to grow in size and become denser than before as if to signal this. Already Bristol seemed much bigger and more important than Coventry.

Jonathan Young

I was attempting to follow my map while at the same, navigate the immediate route ahead. Several times I changed lanes belatedly, realizing that I was in danger of filtering off incorrectly towards another part of town, much to the irritation of those behind me. But at the same time it seemed like I could not get lost even if I wanted to. My car was caught in the steady river of traffic, drawn by an inescapable force towards the centre and the college.

I stopped at one set of traffic lights just long enough to glance around me. To my left was a huge lorry with noisy brakes and a shuddering engine, while to my right a dark blue sports car with blacked out windows and a thumping stereo, awaited its opportunity to overtake me. Across the other side of the junction I could see several huge electricity pylons standing like robotic scarecrows firing energy at the hundreds of buildings around them. *These* other vehicles – this infrastructure – this life, seemed so real – whereas my private musings were fast feeling inconsequential. I needed to pull my socks-up and get on with things. I began to feel like I'd wasted my whole summer.

Without really knowing how I found it, I soon arrived at the college's Halls of Residence. I pulled into the car park and slowed my car to a standstill on the gravely surface below. By now it was late afternoon and I was surprised by the number of people still ferrying bags and boxes to and from the large dormitory building behind. They already seemed to have assembled into small friendship groups of two and three, which I found impressive and slightly daunting given the few hours they could have known each other.

Stepping out of the car, I noticed two attractive looking girls at either end of a large luggage chest that they were helping each other to carry inside. I allowed myself to be curious about who they were - where they were from - where they were going.

This was it. With another large intake of breath I headed in the same direction.

This would be a new chapter. But in many ways it was a chapter that was already written. I'd made up my mind - of course. For the time-being at least, my secret 'double life' would continue. Abandoning my mission at this stage would be failure, or at the very least an embarrassing inconvenience. I wasn't ready for that.

The Edge of Ordinariness

There's no shortage of people in life who seem to want to tell you just *how* to live. Aside from the more established sources of advice on right and wrong, such as parents, school, and church, there are countless less obvious moral guardians. From gossiping busybodies in every corner shop to so-called experts on the radio or TV - they fall over themselves to share their point of view, whether we ask for it or not. The trouble with many of these 'wannabe' standard-bearers is that they are often bedfellows of those transmitting very contrasting messages. At one moment you're told to do the 'right thing,' while at the same time your mind is being stuffed full of thoughts and images that make the exact opposite seem irresistible, often from the same person or place. You can get to the point whereby you just don't know who or what to listen to. It can feel like you've been charged with defending morality by yourself, and picking out a voice of truth from a room full of shouting and scare mongering.

Sex, of course, is a favorite theme for much of this noise.

Sex: scary, frustrating, confusing, exciting, tempting. Sex: so often discussed and so often on your mind, yet in final assessment of your life, perhaps not the demon *or* the problematic mystery you were led to believe. If young Christians are to be tempted to stray from walking the road to righteousness, then sex is the giant billboard that arrests your attention and drags you away. This is what some people would have you believe. This is what some of *them* - the good advice crew — have let sex become.

Edward's Choice

I grew up viewing things slightly differently to this. In many ways I was no less confused, or at risk, than anyone else. But for much of my adolescence, sex was not the goal or preoccupation that it seemed to be for many of my friends. Sure I was intrigued. I shared the physical urges that most kids of my age inevitably felt. But as my parallel 'external' life began to swell more and more, sex actually became a reassuring reference point for me - a landmark at the edge of my Christianity, when many of my personal rules were becoming lost within my burgeoning pretense. Sex — at least going *all the way*, was a line I could not afford to cross; this much was clear to me. If I did, then things would have gone too far. Then I might find that the breadcrumbs leading me back to the *real* Edward had blown away forever.

And for a significant period, this basic tenet of my life gelled well with how I wanted to live. In fact, in many ways it made me feel different and unique. It was like I was carrying a special token of my faith, which would mark me out from other people no matter how things turned out.

In contrast, my friends' obvious desperation to 'get started' with sex was apparent from an early age. Their only obstacle was in finding a partner who was willing to have sex too, and their efforts to overcome this became evident in periods of odd and raw prospecting behavior. Girls would be teased, chased, pushed, groaned at, baited, and begged, as if they were playing out a scene from a wildlife documentary. Most fought back by trying to laugh it off or by simply telling them to grow-up. Others felt humiliated and overwhelmed but still managed to resist. But before long, the boys found more subtle psychological ways to pressurize them, and it became clear that some *were* having sex - either because they wanted to, or because they thought they should. I found many of these situations tragic.

Unfortunately, my actions were often a betrayal of that view, despite hiding from this realization at the time. While I was not 'physically' doing the same thing, I found myself propping up their value system — wanting them to assume that I felt the same way. I'd join in the 'how far did you get' conversations. I even lied about my reasons for finishing different relationships that I had stumbled into, by cruelly reporting back that the girls in question were too frigid or boring to be worth persevering with. I knew, in reality, that many other people weren't actually having sex yet either, but if they suspected that I didn't at least want to dive into this exciting world, then I faced having those same accusations of frigidity thrown at me. I just did not want to stand out as being different.

So I carried on, adding-in more lies and deceit to fill the vacuum created by my secrecy. And in doing so, I systematically undermined the very values my temporary abstinence might otherwise have been testimony to.

Of course, the truth was that *I* was the one who would worry, often prematurely, about how far I might be expected to go with the girls I dated. For this reason, I began most relationships by immediately conjuring up my exit strategy, knowing that I could action this without arousing too much suspicion. Affiliations that lasted no more than a few weeks or days were fairly ordinary at that age and did not attract any criticism.

This shady coping strategy remained in place for most of my time left at school. There were occasions, of course, when I got close to the edge; girls who for different reasons, interested and disturbed me more than the others - who I desperately hoped might want me too. I could not make myself immune to their attractiveness and sometimes felt like sex was the only scale from which to assess how *they* felt. On these few occasions I'd lay awake at night wondering whether I was doing the right thing - reassessing the boundary that I'd set. I'd even go back to scripture and agitatedly check that my stance hadn't all been some big misunderstanding, but found, 1 Corinthians 7:1; "It is good for a man not to touch a woman" - unequivocal. I was looking for loopholes rather than guidance, and subsequently found only roadblocks.

"But I say to the unmarried and to the widows: It is good for them if they remain even as I am" (Corinthians 7:8).

Reading the bible like the safety instructions in a chemistry set only meant that I became disengaged from the words I found within, but at the same time I was still bound by them. And when I was at risk of disobeying, circumstances or perhaps God's timely intervention saved me. On the occasions when I hadn't planned a way to stop things progressing to that stage, something would just happen — like parents unexpectedly returning or other improbable interruptions — to stop it. And, of course, *those* relationships would actually turn out to be something far less significant than I thought they might be at the time. Like anyone, I sometimes felt the pang of disappointment when they ended, but I was able to reflect back that I had been fortunate only weeks later.

The upshot was that I somehow smuggled a view of sex that I saw as unique and precious through to college, and at the time I was pleased it was that way.

Things actually began fairly positively for me there. I shied away from talking to the girls I had noticed in the car park when arriving, but later that same night would be reassured that meeting new people at least, was not going to be such a problem.

Having dumped the bags and boxes from my boot into my rather tired and dingy looking bedroom, I'd followed most of the human traffic towards the student union bar.

Walking in there was an understandably daunting prospect. Despite my earlier mental preparation in the car, I didn't feel ready to trust my powers of conversation initially, so headed directly to get a drink, walking purposefully as if to ward off anyone who might think of approaching me. When I did dare to peek up, my eyes took in what I guess was a fairly typical student bar-room scene — people drinking, chatting, bonding. I was again taken aback by just how well some of them were getting along, given the brief period they could only have known each other. Nearby, a boy and girl hung-off each other flirtatiously, whispering and giggling into each other's ears; and they were not the only ones to appear so intimate.

If I'd felt slightly left behind by how quickly friendships were forming earlier, catching up seemed increasingly unlikely now. To me, the other students even seemed to look older than I was. I was a young kid starting 'big school' all over again, and like then, my mind was conned into awarding the others unwarranted superiority.

I was still processing this information when someone tapped me on the shoulder.

"Hello there, I'm Stuart," boomed a deep voice that was instantly distinguished by a thick west-country tone. At the same time he thrust forward a large right hand for me to shake.

"Good to meet you. This is Steve and Charlie," he continued, temporarily stepping back to allow the others to acknowledge me with a nod.

Stuart was one of those people who actually passed as several years older, even when you got to know him. It wasn't just the fact that he was so tall. Beneath the faded Rugby shirt he wore tonight, he had the expanding body of someone who might easily be middle-aged. The youthful exception to his overall appearance was an expectant stare that drew your conversation, like an inquisitive child probing you for information. Stuart was a genuinely friendly guy and an extrovert. The fact he was still eagerly working to introduce himself to new people, having already gained Steve and Charlie for company that evening, was testimony to this.

The rest of the conversation progressed as you might expect: "Where are you from...What are you here to study... What sport do you like...We're off into town for a few drinks later, fancy joining us?"

And I did join them. In fact, I spent quite a large part of those first few weeks with Stuart, Steve, and Charlie. Although we did not discover many things we had in common right away, they were basically good guys and useful companions to pick through the awkward college familiarization process with. Stuart in particular would willingly dip his toe into the water first with regard to most of

Edward's Choice

the early challenges we faced: how to enroll, where to eat, how to loan money. He was such a 'big' character in every way, that he seemed inevitably to encounter these issues before the rest of us, and was more than happy to share what he learned.

But perhaps because we were very different people, or because they just didn't fit the expectations of the people I'd meet that I'd established before arriving, I'd never come to feel that our friendship moved beyond a fairly basic level. I wanted someone to come into my life and affect me in the same way the likes of David, Sam, or even Jared had. Stuart and the others were friends, but through no fault of their own, they just weren't the ones to provide the direction that I was looking for.

So in those initial days, a large part of me just went on looking and waiting. And as each day passed without this deeper companionship, my 'positive' start began to flake away and then crack. It was *that* growing sense of loneliness that became an environment for doubts to germinate and then grow about me – doubts about where it was all going - how capable I was of fitting in. Though I sometimes remembered to pray, they were often prayers of anxiety and pleading, rather than ones of genuine belief. Because of this, it was a period that saw me becoming steadily more desperate. I was ready to recognize almost anyone as the saviour that I needed.

The Australians turned up at about two weeks after the rest of us – and immediately changed everything. Like one of those water-filled ornaments that you shake to create a snowy scene, they unsettled the calm order and pattern of the previous weeks, and kicked up a storm of re-integration all over again.

It would be oversimplifying things to say that this was just because they were more sociable, or for some reason, louder than the rest of us. Equally, this could not be completely attributed to the intrigue around their nationality - other students arrived from all over Europe as well as Canada without creating the same impression. What they had – collectively and for the most part individually

— was a charismatic quality and attitude that propelled them prominence within that little world. Even compared to Stuart, who until now had perhaps been one of the most high profile people on campus, people were compelled to notice them.

I found out later that the two girls — Imogen and Kate — along with Kevin, who attended many of the same classes as me, were from Canberra. The final two members of the group, Nikos and Blake, were from just outside Melbourne. It was Blake more than anyone, who defined the rest with his strong and commanding personality. They would all be staying for around six months, but this didn't deter anyone from investing time in getting to know them.

You could tell when they were around. In the canteen at meal times it felt like all the other students were either trying to talk to them, or just watching them - like they were some sort of celebrities.

Blake in particular, became like a pied piper figure for the boys on campus and had set up an unofficial 'Australian Rules' football team within days. I suspected that the majority of the players were not particularly interested in the sport itself, but knew that participating would put them close to *him* and consequently at the epicenter of the college social scene. Even for those of us who remained on the outside of things, it was difficult to ignore completely. Practice would take place on the field just outside the two halls of residence, and the loud shouts that accompanied the game easily pervaded the bedroom windows to disturb us.

Because of this, and possibly because I was slightly jealous of them, the Australians were initially a source of mild irritation to me. But other than this, for those first few weeks I did not get close enough to them to form much of an opinion either way. I was also pretty certain that they were unaware of me. But this would not be the case for long.

I eventually stumbled onto their radar as a result of getting to know Kevin. On the third or fourth occasion he turned up for my class on contemporary novels, we struck up a conversation and ended up getting along fairly well. He introduced me to the rest of the gang – including Kate, that same night. It was Halloween.

I had arrived at the student union bar with Stuart – although given the self-transformation he had effected in the hours before – he was now firmly in the role of Frankenstein's monster. The posters that had been dotted around the campus had instructed 'Halloween Disco – come in costume,' and Stuart, being the type of guy who instinctively wanted to support such *fun* initiatives, was more than happy to comply. The basis of his costume was a long tight fitting suit that could easily have been worn by a member of the *Adams Family*. He had combed his hair tightly to one side, whitened his face, and to complete the look, attached two plastic bolts that he had bought from a fancy dress shop in town, to either side of his head. He looked fantastic.

I, on the other hand, had never really gone in for celebrating Halloween, and had barely made the effort tonight. I had covered my face with the same white face-paint, thrown on an old torn shirt, and styled my hair to point up in various directions, with a view to passing off as a generic zombie or ghoul. Looking at myself in the mirror before I left my room, I had actually begun to worry whether anyone would in fact recognize I was in costume or instead just assume I was looking scruffy and slightly ill.

Led by Kevin, the rest of the Aussies had come over to where we were standing soon after arriving themselves. Stuart's costume had already drawn several admiring glances and giggles, but even in this respect it seemed he would be overshadowed by *them*. Imogen, dressed as a 'devil women' - complete with horns, a red-cape, fish-net tights, and long red boots – had instantly wrestled away the attention of most people there as she walked across the room. It was a pretty unoriginal outfit, but one she carried off well, and even as Kevin introduced Stuart and I to the others, a small group of the bravest boys had already begun congregating around.

Perhaps choosing to interpret this as some sort of territorial challenge, it wasn't long before Blake moved across to act as Imogen's chaperone, and was soon dominating that exchange in the way he bossed most conversations. At the same time, Stuart had begun enthusiastically chatting to Kevin and Nikos, leaving me, by default, alone with Kate.

"Hi Eddy - we've not met properly," she began. I felt sure because she felt obliged to fill the silence.

"Yeah, hi. I think my room is just above yours – on the next floor up, obviously." It was a slightly odd thing to say, and I blushed at my own stupidity.

She did me a favor by ignoring it, instead choosing to comment on my appearance.

"If you don't mind me saying Ed, your costume looks a little – well, underdone."

"Right," I replied, sulkily.

Kate was definitely the least imposing of the Australians, and someone who was quite difficult to read. She smiled infrequently and I learned over time that her expressions generally gave away little about how she was feeling. It was almost as if she had been calibrated to react to the things that happened to her at a different level to everyone else. In a strange way this was part of her attractiveness. It made you want to try even harder to invoke some sort of emotional response from her. But here, on the first occasion, she smiled with very little prompting from me.

It instantly improved my mood.

"Well, I've seen more convincing witches," I retorted, assured that it was appropriate for me to join in the teasing.

"How rude," she said – giggling now.

"Well my costume may not be too hot, but my spells are pretty wicked, so watch out."

"I will," I said.

I was both agitated and excited by talking to her. Although I told myself I was imagining it, all my senses shouted out that she was flirting with me. I quickly felt an irrational sense of nervousness, as if I had finally been given a chance to prove I could make it there at college, but only had this one night to do it. It was almost a relief when Kate disappeared onto the dance floor. I headed towards where Stuart was standing at the bar, with the intention of drowning these disquieting thoughts with lager.

But the drink, of course, would only serve to drive my curiosity — daring me to prove that there was substance to the softness and interest I thought I had detected. This was suppose to be *my* new life, but until now I had spent the whole of my time at Bristol feeling like a spectator, waiting and watching others from the sidelines. What had I to lose? I drank what was left in my glass and took, what was for me, the fairly rare step of walking onto the dance-floor heading towards where *they* were. I was no dancer, but I hoped the dense crowd would mask my ungainliness.

Moving through the mesh of bodies was like riding on a ghost train. As I brushed past them, every now and then the aggravated face of a wizard, ghoul, or ogre would turn slowly into the light to face me, before mechanically moving back and disappearing in the broader throng of revelers. I was disoriented - lost within this monster's ball. Until suddenly, I felt a Devil's fork poke me in the back.

It wasn't Imogen. The prop had become separated from its owner and it was now in the possession of Kate who was creating her own mischief. Having got my attention she quickly wedged her body between me and the person behind, still somehow finding the room to twist her hips and raise her arms to the music.

I could not be sure whether I was dancing too, or just standing there numbly. I felt a lump come to my throat. The lights flashed on and off now, casting the whole dance-floor into darkness, before bathing it again in red, yellow, or green, and making it seem like Kate's body jolted magically into the next dance pose without physically moving in between. But every time the light returned, it was clear that her eyes remained fixed hypnotically upon mine. There could be no mistaking her attention now.

We danced for a while longer - I'm not sure how long. But almost as if Kate used her spell again to transport us both to a later point in the night, without really knowing how I found myself pinned against the railings outside being kissed. It was a passionate kiss. She burrowed her fingers into the back of my neck and pressed herself heavily against me. I was overwhelmed by a sense of unpreparedness, fear even, and my heart pounded as if it might outgrow my torso. But at the same time I felt better than I had done for weeks. I was suddenly alive.

Without warning, Kate wriggled from my embrace and led me by the hand towards our hall of residence.

It was then, suddenly, all those feelings were replaced by cold realization. I'd been here before. It was that same sense of alarm and lack of control that I'd experienced before. Without any sign of it coming, my desire to somehow get a foothold in this life – the life that was going on all around me, had been answered by Kate. She had somehow smuggled me in among the shadows. Now I was afraid that I would be expected to legitimize my presence there by going all the way with her. It seemed like my values were slipping out of my grasp before I had thought to clench my fingers. As my thoughts breathlessly caught up with this reality, I began to contemplate an embarrassing U-turn or actually stepping over that boundary.

I'm not sure which way this would have gone. The dilemma was still frantically washing around my head when we reached the landing next to the stairs on her floor. But to my relief, *she* took away the crisis from my mind almost as quickly as she had created it.

"We'll leave things there for tonight," she said, planting a rushed and conclusive kiss on my lips.

"Besides, I have a witch's broth to get back to," she added.

"Right," I replied.

That night I wandered off to my room feeling like I'd been talked into a skydive, only for it to be canceled at the last minute.

I was pleased by that sudden turn of events, but at the same time elated by what had happened up until that point. I was also curious to understand what it all meant to her. Indeed, as I lay in bed retracing the whole thing later, I'd find myself looking for clues. Was what happened spontaneous or had she planned it? Had she changed her mind about me so quickly? Did she sense *my* uneasiness? These and other questions stumbled around my head in the same way I imagined the last lonely ghosts and demons stumbling restlessly back from the bar; until eventually they were suppressed and then overcome by sleep.

Without any classes to go to, I allowed myself to sleep-in and arrived down at breakfast late the next morning. By now the majority of students had trudged off to lectures or back to bed, and I sat down to my plate of beans on toast, alone. I began thinking about Kate. Not quite with the troubled emphasis I had tried to recall the night's events the previous evening, but just allowing the memory of her speaking to me to fill my mind.

To my surprise, the recollection of her voice was superseded by the real thing entering my consciousness.

"Give it back would you?" I heard from across the room.

She had just walked into the canteen with the rest of the Australians and was shouting towards Blake. Along with Nikos, he was simulating a sword-fight using the long plastic tubes that some students used to carry their Art coursework around. Judging by Kate's reaction, the tube that Blake was using for his weapon had been stolen from her.

For some reason, at this point, I didn't feel ready to speak to her. I hadn't had the chance to think about what *I* actually wanted and having that next conversation with her now, in front of them, would feel like I was allowing them all to feast on my discomfort and uncertainty. I wished there were more people around so that I might merge in amongst them - out of sight.

Having grown tired of their initial game, Blake and Nikos were soon trying to goad Kate more directly by flinging her tube to and fro over her head. Their efforts seemed wasted. Far from being affected by their teasing, her face was expressionless, like she might be reading a book or choosing from a menu, and other than the odd request for it to be returned, she seemed to have little motivation to retrieve or intercept her property.

Just when I thought they might move through without noticing me there, Nikos missed his catch and the tube came flying down towards where I was sitting. Blake bounded down to collect it.

"Hey Kate, have a look who's here," came the excitable shout as I was discovered.

Blake picked up the tube and prodded me on the back with it, as if to emphasize my whereabouts. It was done playfully, but with much greater force than was necessary. I was annoyed but tried not to show it.

"Is there room for us to join you?"

I knew he was poking fun at the fact I was sitting alone, but it was also quickly apparent, that I wasn't the one he really wanted to wind-up. I was merely more ammunition in his campaign against Kate.

"Why don't you come and say hello to your new friend," he said, probably expecting her to feel the awkwardness and ignore his request.

As usual though, Kate seemed to revel in defying predictability, and did just as Blake instructed, offering a quick "Hi" in my direction, before pushing past him to find a chair immediately to my right. Blake pursed his lips together in a reluctant and irritated smile.

Nikos, Kevin, and Imogen soon sat down too, and after a few more minutes, beckoned over two of the people that *were* still in the room to join us, as if to re-emphasize their popularity. All this time, Blake continued to stare at us like an incensed animal watching a predator circle its young. But the noise created by the additional people, meant that we could briefly share a few words without being heard by them.

"They're going clubbing in town tonight. I'm going to say that I'm feeling sick.

Come round to my room, won't you?"

I was left dumbstruck by the weight and directness of the question, and couldn't initially find anything to say.

Although he could not have known what she had said, Blake was suddenly out of his seat, as if it had become unbearably hot.

"God I'm bored. Let's get out of here. You coming?" he said to them all, but looking directly at Kate.

She went on, ignoring him.

"So what do you say? Are you going to humiliate a girl by declining?" she whispered to me.

It was a potentially embarrassing question and situation for her, but she delivered the words without a hint of stress or anxiety.

"Kate, c'mon," Blake shouted — even more crossly now.

"Yeah, of course I'll come," I replied at last.

"About nine — no earlier."

Everything that had happened in those past few hours had been unanticipated and overwhelming to me. And yet, given my increasingly brittle self-confidence, I should not have been surprised by how intoxicating I had found it all. I was confused and finding it hard to reconcile the life I wanted to live with the puzzling realities that confronted me at college. The notion that someone could make it all fit together was so easy to fall in love with.

Things had moved quickly - too quickly for me to rationalize, but during the next few hours, I'd have time to carefully consider the implications of it all. I had the opportunity to think about where it was all heading, and even make myself responsible for what might take place. And so I posed myself questions like: Did I really like her? Could I be sure about her based on the brief time we'd had together so far? Could this be what God intended?

Slowly – unjustifiably – I'd begin to find ways of convincing myself that the answer could be 'yes.'

I tried to remember the things she'd done so far, which I might use to substantiate it. I even dared to imagine her being a secret agent herself - an angel sent by God to shelter and keep me. And if *this* wasn't to be, I hoped for something that would give me more time. Perhaps the norms for relationships in Australia were different and she might share my hesitancy regarding sex. *That* could be the reason she hadn't let things go further the previous evening.

Deep down, I knew even then that my thought process was illogical, but I had tasked my mind to come up with the reasoning to support my decision, and these were the only crumbs of hope it could find.

I would go to her room, and whether I was being foolish or not, over those hours I slowly began to find ways to put my faith into a stranger. Even if my improbable notions of what Kate's stance would be did prove groundless, would it be so wrong for *that* to happen? Seeing the way sex was such a normal part of life there at college during those weeks had made the idea of waiting to be married seem absurd. I was finding it ever more difficult to believe that everyone had got it so wrong, and I was right. What if the opposite was true? Perhaps my beliefs had become mixed-up and distorted during those years of secrecy. Wasn't it just time to grow-up and leave my hang-ups behind?

A few hours later I sat watching as the last digit of my alarm clock altered and the time changed to '21:04.' I stood up ready to make my way down to Kate's room. In truth, I had been waiting and watching that clock so closely during the last thirty minutes that by now my eyes seemed to be playing tricks on me. The figures somehow seemed unreliable in how quickly they were updating and even lacked conviction about which number they should transfer to. Even their reality appeared uncertain.

I barely had a chance to knock on the door when Kate pulled it open and beckoned me over the threshold. Her room was filled with cushions and other furnishings that made it look generally more comfortable than my own, and the scent and light emitted from several candles she had lit, enhanced this sense of coziness. She led me by the hand to sit on her bed. Kate usually wore her hair tied-neatly back, but tonight, auburn strands fell over her face, making her appear less guarded and calculating somehow, than she could often seem to be. I hoped that finally I'd get a chance to see through her mystery – that there would be hidden depths and secrets that would mean, even now, I could be saved again.

I was still unsure about the whole situation, but I didn't feel nervous now. I even wanted to tell Kate about my mind's relentless debate, feeling that she could make sense of it. So often since, I've daydreamed about how things might have turned out if I had.

Instead though, we kissed; in a way that was softer than the evening before. The pace suggested we had more time, like I'd joined her on a slow comfortable ride to somewhere inevitable.

"Kate this is great - you are great," I said, still needing something from her to be sure, "but you're not going to be around for long are you?"

"Shushh," she whispered, choosing not to answer.

Instead, she poured us both a glass of red wine. None of this was done dismissively. It was more a case of her selfishly protecting these moments – our moments. I knew that my own tendency to over-analyze things could strangle life and stop it from just being.

Conceding this to myself, I exhaled heavily as if to let go of my troubles, and lay forward on her bed. She began to massage my shoulders.

"Ed, you seem so lost and mixed up. It's adorable, but please relax - because I'm going to look after you."

I wished I could look at her to see the truth in her eyes.

"Really?"

This time, choosing not to answer verbally, she stopped the massage to trace out the letters 'Y-E-S' on my back with her finger.

I felt convinced. But one more time I asked her for reassurance, now prepared to believe anything she would tell me:

"Kate, is there anyway you could stay longer? How long do you think you could stay?"

Somehow, if she could satisfy me on this, then we had a chance. Then *it* would be alright.

Again, she responded by gently writing out the letters on my back: 'F-O-R-E-V-E-R.'

And that was it. Satisfied with this as my contract, I gave myself up to her. She gave herself up to me. And finally, I felt like I belonged to the world.

When it was over, I just laid there. I wanted more than anything to talk to her, but instead I stared quietly into the darkness, hardly even allowing my breath to disturb the silence. I wondered whether she was asleep.

How could she sleep? I needed her. I needed her to stay awake with me all night so that she might protect me from the morning and all its implications. I wondered whether *I* would sleep at all.

But I must have done so, because in the early hours of the morning I was awoken by her. She nudged me, while at the same time, passing me my T-shirt to put on.

"You should leave. I mean - you can stay, but the guys normally call in on me in the morning and it will be difficult for you."

It was like a siren puncturing my dream — a dream that I was exactly the same person as the day before. I quickly gathered up the rest of my clothing, got dressed and left.

I spent most of the next day feeling strangely numb. It was a Friday, and although this time I *did* have lectures to go to, I decided to stay in my room through the morning anyway. My state of mind was that of someone who was resigned to receiving bad news. It was like I'd been convinced to swallow a pill that had made the world fall in love with me for one night, but now would slowly make me ugly in the eyes of God. Between television programs that I wasn't really watching, I stood up to look at the mirror, half expecting my features to start mutating in some way. Of course, nothing happened.

But something *was* changing — something far closer to my core. Looking back, if the whole experience with Kate was to bring one realization into stark perspective — it was how the lies you live and tell often find their way into truth.

Somewhere in my heart, I probably knew that God's love was still with me — even if I dare not expect or rely on it at this point. My life wasn't ruined and I didn't feel evil. I didn't even feel especially guilty or bad. I just felt ordinary. It was as if I was turning into one of those people back at school who had made having sex their goal, just because convention said they should. I was becoming the person I'd spent the last years pretending to be. I was becoming ordinary. And I would soon be made to feel even more ordinary.

This interpretation hung around me like a relentless insect and the only way I could think of escaping it, was to let my curiosity about how Kate might be feeling takeover for a time. Her part in this had almost become a secondary consideration for me since, but I had staked so much on her and needed to know whether *that* trust would be rewarded. I'd actually been glad to leave her room earlier that morning, but now I allowed myself to feel bothered by why she had asked me to go.

These thoughts were the spur I needed to force me up and out of my room. Shaking away the sense of lethargy that had mired my morning, I threw on some clothes and made my way to the door hoping to find both the answers and reassurance I was looking for.

At times those corridors in the Halls of Residence were bristling with life and activity, but that day they were almost empty and soundless. The only students

Jonathan Young

I came across seemed to be moving purposefully about their business alone, in the same way I imagined monks methodically wandering to their tasks in a large silent monastery. It was only when I arrived at the bottom of the stairs that I heard the sound of shouting outside.

It occurred to me that it was probably a game of Aussie rules football that was being played on the lawn. *She* was likely to be among those watching. I had become quite proud of my record of defiance in never having joined in or watched one of those games, but now I reluctantly decided to back-down on my stance.

It was a cold clear day outside, and I felt the low winter sun kissing my neck as I walked out. There were fewer spectators than I'd anticipated, and the sight of their breath in the chilly air made them look like chimneys positioned sporadically around the make-shift pitch. As I'd anticipated, Kate was one of them.

Would she come over? I was worried that the low sun behind me would make me just another silhouette that was indistinguishable from the other figures that stood around. Not knowing whether to approach her or not, I decided to hang around there for a few minutes before deciding what to do.

Happily her attention fixed on me for a second in a way that suggested I'd been noticed, and she soon walked over to stand by my side. Still watching the game, she began our conversation in a 'matter-of-fact' tone, as if she might be updating me on the play I'd missed.

"Hi."

"Hi."

"You okay?"

"Yeah."

"Listen, sorry about this morning."

"No, don't worry about it."

There was nothing particularly missing from the words themselves, but I drew no confidence at all from how they were delivered. I needed more from her. But instead, what little substance there was to our relationship began to bleed away.

"Ed, listen, I wanted to talk."

"Yeah, me too."

"Please, let me go first. Ed, I had a good time last night, but Blake and I have been sort of, on and off since we arrived here, and I think maybe we're going to give it another go."

Each word now was like a boulder plunged upon my chest, making it harder and harder to breathe.

I somehow coughed out the words, "right. Okay."

"I'm sorry."

"No really, I'm okay."

But I wasn't okay. I new things like this happen, but until now, they didn't happen to me.

I'm not certain how that conversation ended. I'm sure I played my part in it like a telephone message system, unconsciously going through its program of responses, but mentally I had already pulled myself out of the firing line, perhaps realizing that everything I remembered about it would be poisonous to me later.

Afterwards, I walked away until I felt I was out of Kate's sight, and then ran as fast as I could away from there. And I carried on running across the campus for some distance - only stopping to lean on a wall when I felt I might be sick. I didn't even try to understand the consequences of it all immediately. But I knew that it was bad, and that later, my mind *would* demand an inquest.

The hurt would come along first. It was a physical as well as a mental sensation — as if my heart had been stripped of its supporting muscle and tissue and was laid bare to the air. I'm not sure that I had convinced myself that I loved her or anything like that, but in many ways I felt ready to love, and this made what she had done seem even more unfair and incomprehensible.

And then afterwards, those feelings soon gave way to anger and confusion. Nothing about it added up. Part of me wanted to storm back to Kate to demand a better explanation. How could she have done this to me - she had said forever? How could God have let me be duped in that way?

Of course I knew that actually going back there would only lead to more humiliation. So instead I spent the next couple of hours on the shuttle bus that ferried students between the four college sites in the city, riding aimlessly around, and allowing myself to wallow and dwell on these thoughts for a while.

In a strange way, there was something about feeling that way that suited me. I knew that this pain was a counterbalance to the concern and regret I might otherwise be experiencing, because of what Kate and I had done. I hadn't wanted to be rejected in that way, but now I had, I subconsciously hoped the whole scenario might prove to be my trade-off with God. Just like in those years before I had really understood forgiveness, I hoped this pain – the injustice of it all, might just persuade Him not to punish me again. I hoped it meant I could go on being His secret agent.

For a while afterwards, it seemed life would just move on. I resisted any temporary inclination to leave college that I may have had, and as a distraction, even paid more attention to my studies. Stuart and the others must also have had some vague awareness of what happened, as during those same few days they made a point of dragging me everywhere like a child they had been given the job of minding. Their efforts to include me were fairly clumsy, but still appreciated - especially given that I'd been a less than model friend to them recently.

Over the following weeks my confidence slowly returned, and even withstood the odd encounter with Kate. On those occasions we bumped into each other, we shared fairly meaningless and empty conversations that probably said little about what either of us were thinking. With each meeting, my disappointment lessened and I overcame my longing to spot signs of lingering attachment between us.

More significantly for me, I began to think about my life as a Christian again. I was sorry for having been angry with God, and knew that I had been wrong. Having slept with Kate, I was now in new territory – past the point where I still believed I had the right to count myself as one of His followers. For this reason, when I tentatively began thumbing my way through the Bible again, it was like I was a prisoner peering through a cell window at the sunshine and scenery outside. I knew I'd taken a first dangerous step down a path that Paul warned would lead to a 'debased mind' (Romans 1:28), and while I wanted to revisit His words, I wasn't immediately ready to contemplate the great gifts I read about as being available to me.

But the thing is, the more I read, the less sure I became that my cell was even locked. Nothing that I found there seemed to suggest that I had messed-up in a way that meant I would never be able to recover. Slowly – very slowly, and without really knowing why initially, I began to believe that I had not forfeited my right to a Christian life after all.

Despite this, the events of those few days wouldn't simply recede into memories without leaving their mark upon me. The way I interpreted all about me had shifted by a few degrees – my eyes had been opened. An immunity to the world's fixation with sex that I had always credited myself with, had been scratched away, and over the ensuing years I became more aware of it. It seemed more culpable to its basest forms wherever they were found - magazines, films, television - in life. I'd kid with myself that it didn't matter, as long as my thoughts didn't translate into me making the same mistake again, but I was like an alcoholic trying to ignore a bottle hidden away in my house. My heart was already darkening.

"The lamp of the body is the eye. Therefore, when your eye is good, your whole body also is full of light. But when your eye is bad, your body also is full of darkness" (Luke 11:34-35).

And it would continue to darken. Predictably, when my life faltered again during those years, this would often be the theme.

So at the end of it all, did I learn where the edge of ordinariness was? If I were to live through those days again now, would I know everything I needed to about Christianity and sex?

In many ways, rather than helping me to find the answers I was looking for, the whole experience helped me understand that I'd been asking the wrong questions.

It showed me that my naive interpretation of what sex was all about in the years leading up to college, was probably just as flawed as the compromised beliefs that left me dipping in and out of sin afterwards. Sex had become like a theme of my Christian life – a line that I was determined not to step over. Sadly, I became so obsessed with hiding my intentions – acting my way through the scenes of my adolescence in a way that made me fit neatly within the world, that when I looked down at the grass about my feet, it had become overgrown and the line seemed less distinguishable.

It also showed me that many of those people who want to tell you how to live your life, often don't even come close to depicting the true complexity of what it's really like. It's easy to point out where others are going wrong. It's all too easy to look back and cringe embarrassingly at the mistakes you walked straight into yourself. But at the time, there is a life there and you have little choice but to live it. When it happens – when temptation calls, it's often when you're feeling at your most vulnerable - when you need more than anything else for someone to rescue you from uncertainty, loneliness, and tell you everything is going to be okay.

Because of this, all that good advice can start to feel like a set of instructions tossed around in a phony war - 'Don't have sex,' 'Be careful,' 'Only have sex when...' There's no wonder young people can feel in crisis regarding sex when it's so tied up in secrecy, myth, convention, exaggeration, shame, and emotion - whether they approach this as Christians or not.

For this reason, sex can be a cruel awakening - a disappointment that you often only truly start to appreciate in the moments after it has happened. But it can also be a wonderful gift that underpins the most permanent and perfect of unions. This is how He intended it. So rather spending time assessing what the boundaries are, or worrying about what *they* say, I think its much more important that you are prepared to find the answers you need in faith and love.

If you listen hard enough, and you are truly prepared to believe what you hear, that's the truth you'll pick out above all the other noise.

Going Native

It's clear, at times I've let myself down. I've overestimated myself and begun thinking I can plot a way through this life to heaven alone. I've lost control - crashed, and when realization takes hold, it can be like splinters piercing your skin. The last thing you want to do at such times is face your Saviour.

The last thing you want to do is put your wretchedness before His perfection. It's easier to close your eyes and sink back beneath the covers. Sitting in darkness, deferring life, being alone – has sometimes felt like the only option for me. That was until He picked me up again.

On dozens of occasions, this feeling of despondency has travelled in among the pain and nausea of a quarrelling hangover. While on the general scale of drunken behaviour, mine might not be judged as anything too special, I've said the wrong thing to the wrong person, upset too many friends, let slip too many secrets and woken up in the wrong place enough times for it to have become a bit of a problem. You see, when your starting point is that, a few beers might be a good way of fitting in with a more secular crowd, believing in a much longer term plan of somehow introducing people to Christianity - this sort of thing is just not supposed to happen.

Sometimes, when you are working for God's secret army, you go so far undercover that you actually forget your mission. This started to happen to me more and more. And whether I admitted it or not - more and more this would begin after a couple of drinks.

It can start harmlessly enough. A few years later I was working for a marketing agency, and joined up with some colleagues one night to celebrate a promotion that one of them had just been given.

In truth, at the time it was fairly typical for a dozen or so of us to head into town from our Birmingham office after work on a Friday evening, whether there was reason to celebrate or not. Special occasions such as this, merely meant that a few more people tagged along than normal.

At this stage in my life I inexplicably found myself attaching a disproportionate sense of hope to such nights. Without any real justification, they somehow felt like a gateway to new relationships and possibilities. It was like jumping into a pool of a hundred people and a hundred conversations - and in amongst the small-talk, the chat-up lines, the gossip and the laughter, I felt there might just be something or someone there to change things for me in a positive way.

It was with this sense of optimism that I first stepped onto the lift and then strode out of the big revolving door at the front of the building where we worked, along with two guys from my department. It was mid-June and the type of sunny day that improves your mood as soon as you walk out into the warm infusing air.

After just a few minutes, we were in the city centre and walking between groups of friends as they sat coolly sipping beer and wine around the tables that aligned the different bars and pubs. Today more than ever, it seemed that everywhere you turned there were attractive and stylishly-dressed people with sophisticated looking lives. They were immaculate - almost as if the pages from a fashion magazine or catalogue might have been draped across the street to create the scene. It was impossible for me not to find this world desirable.

In amongst it all, we soon found the familiar faces of the rest of our friends. Several stacks of empty glasses revealed that they had started the evening in eager fashion.

"Scott, Ravi, Eddy...where have you lot been?" they greeted us, kicking back chairs for us to sit down.

"Drinks? You're up for a big-one tonight eh?" said Tony, the most gregarious of the boys.

And those words signalled the start of the night and a journey that would unfortunately expose my fragility again.

Although I had been in the job for around five months, even now I felt such occasions had value in cementing my sense of belonging with my workmates. While most of the people here shared flats or houses in Birmingham, I was still *in the process* of moving out of my parents' house in Coventry. For some reason this sometimes made me feel like I was outside of the core group, or having to try harder than the others to fit in. There were some imposing characters here, and I was fairly desperate for them to like me, but more than that, they were also gatekeepers to my plan – and to this enchanting part of society.

Of course, at this stage of early adulthood, socializing like that hardly felt like a choice – it was more of a cultural norm. I was aware that these weren't the most Christian of surroundings, but trying to avoid this would have felt like I was placing unreasonable limitations on those people available to me to interact with - like somehow pretending the real world and its varied and rich fruits were not out there to be sampled.

Here tonight, I was definitely opting-in. Before long, I began talking to a girl called Jude who worked in the public relations division of my company. Until now, my impression of her was of someone who was inaccessible to most of us – typically spending her days having important telephone conversations, rushing to catch trains to London, or 'doing' lunch with journalists. She was pretty in a conventional way, and well-dressed in a dark expensive looking trouser-suit, denoting that she certainly did not look out of place in this trendy part of town. During our conversation, I found myself lying to her about having eaten at an expensive restaurant in Chelsea that she had referred to. I was also delighted when she giggled when I made a joke about one of the company bosses, and went on to ask me about a project at work that I was involved with.

Our chat — which quickly began to feel like a success, and the beers I had drank, soon contributed to a sense of confidence that was now swelling inside of me. It was like I had started to access a powerful well in my mind that transformed me into a much more social animal and turned on the taps of my conversation. Even if I had not been to that restaurant, I came to think that it was the type of place I might easily visit. More and more, I felt convincing enough to be in this environment and with these people.

We were interrupted by Tony's invitation to join in with a drinking game that he was trying to get going. At this stage I was no more than tipsy, and I'd not really started out on such nights with the sole objective of getting drunk for a long time. These days, my most unruly and embarrassing moments usually occurred as a by-product of an evening's excesses, rather than being the intended end point. Unfortunately, Tony's games *were* creatively designed specifically to speed up the intoxication process. Moreover, like many things he said, his words were delivered in a way that presumed our participation.

In reality things infrequently got out of hand amongst us, but the values of an excessive drinking culture were lorded and perpetuated here. I knew that I'd reach my own drinking limit relatively quickly, but for those with a much greater capacity for alcohol consumption, a boisterous - if superficial reverence often awaited. People like Tony who was high up on the food chain in this regard - enjoyed a notable reputation for his ability to guzzle an extraordinary number of pints, even if most people awarded their praise without any aspirations to achieve the same status.

It was no surprise that he was the instigator here. My mistake was to go along with things, fearing that choosing not to participate might make me look like a killjoy or coward.

I would be made to pay. Even though Tony's first offering was essentially a game of chance, based around *paper, scissors, and stone*, I somehow contrived to lose my personal contest with the guy sitting to my right almost every time my turn came around. On each occasion, my penalty was to quickly drink a quantity of lager roughly measured by three of my fingers across my pint glass.

And things would get worse. The next game was more testing and involved trying to add up the value of coins thrown into an ashtray by the participants, as we moved clockwise around the table, with the third person in the sequence each time having to shout-out the running total. Aside from losing your loose change to the person who preceded you, the consequence of demonstrating poor mental arithmetic was to knock back one of several shots Tony had eagerly produced from the bar. This was complicated further by a host of sub-rules based on the players' actions, such as ensuring you weren't the last person to touch your nose when someone would silently initiate this odd ritual around the table - with failure carrying the same price.

I tried desperately to focus my increasingly chaotic thoughts on following both streams of the contest, but was again an early loser. And the harder I tried, the more I was inclined to miss something. I could not be sure, but I sensed that people's eyes began to fix on me, eagerly waiting for my next mistake. And with this thought, blood began to rush to my head and I panicked even more.

I again tried to keep trace of the numbers, while I privately pleaded for a reprieve.

'Forty-eight, fifty-three - not me again, please not me again - sixty-three.'

Yet I seemed destined to be the one to slip-up and pay the forfeit on a frequent basis. In fact, around five more times.

Eventually the game seemed to lose momentum as the players ran out of the necessary coins and motivation to carry on. I knew I had come off much worse than anybody else, and hoped my deteriorating state-of-mind and growing feeling of giddiness was not as obvious to everyone else as it was to me.

Although I briefly tried to pick-up where I had left off in my conversation with

Edward's Choice

Jude, she seemed distracted and less engaged now. I also noticed a small smile come across her face, which I agitatedly surmised must be in response to my words becoming slurred or my eyes moving lazily, betraying my drunkenness. Whereas I felt I was striking a real chord with her before, something was undermining me now.

And yet despite this, I still thought I could be okay. Although things had spiralled temporarily out of my control, I believed I could conceal the sense of agitation and incapacity that was gripping me. If I could just hold myself together, I could rescue things with Jude, and go on to make the right impression with other people that were around. There could perhaps still be something in this night for me.

But there's always a tipping point.

"C'mon lets go - we're moving on," shouted Tony.

By now he had unbuttoned his shirt down to just above his stout stomach and was sweating profusely. He had himself passed the point of censoring any of the comments that he made to the rest of us, and was trying to assert his role as unofficial leader by noisily hogging the conversation and bossing the rest of us around. Increasingly, he also sought to make fun at the expense of others around the table. For this reason, he would truly revel in what came next.

As I moved to stand up, I missed the corner of my chair with what was supposed to be my weight bearing left hand, and slipped backwards onto the table. The sound of several glasses smashing and our drink tray clattering upon the ground, provided the fairly stock confirmation that a minor bar-room incident – with me at its centre – was taking place, and instantly drove my sense of personal crisis to a new level.

"W' hey, Eddy – that's what I like to see," said Tony.

"Steady-on mate," came another voice, more tensely.

For two or three seconds every head in the bar seemed to look towards me – some laughing, some adopting more surprised and disapproving expressions. Two of my workmates nervously tried to help me navigate by the rest of the tables into the open street.

"I'm okay – just leave me," I said sharply.

When we had finally vacated the scene, some of my friends began to see the lighter side of what had gone on. One of the blokes I was with slapped me supportively on the back, while Tony and another boy went on chuckling annoyingly for several minutes. Others, sensitively suggested that this might be a good time for me to go home. Despite the fact I was feeling more drunk with each passing moment, I found all these reactions irritating and excessive in different ways. I was still convinced that it was just an unfortunate accident, and resolved to carry on and prove I was okay.

As much as I felt they were all being unreasonable, I desperately wanted to earn their trust again. I knew I had so much to do now.

Having made it into the next bar, I stumbled into the washrooms and stood alone for a while in one of the cubicles. There, I stared jadedly into the toilet – trying to sift through the hazy images of the night so far, and find the formula for recovery – as the outline of my own reflection slowly came in and out of focus in the bowl below. My head started to fill up with questions: Was Jude laughing with them? Just how much of an idiot had I looked?

In a strange way, tonight now seemed so vital. It was as if the difficulties and the struggles of my whole life were being recounted and paraded before me. Although I knew that Jude did not really mean anything to me, somehow failing to make her and the others like me this evening seemed to mean I'd go on failing. The desire to make things right – finding what I needed – began to feel like a desperate thirst. Everything else - God, my faith, and my mission, slipped further and further into the periphery of my consciousness.

And that was it. Just a few years into that 'long-term' plan of somehow fitting in, I had well and truly become consumed by the process. For me, this was the furthest place on earth from heaven and is somewhere that I've unfortunately visited again many times.

Of course, we all have moments we are not proud of – events that we prefer not to be reminded of. But at this time in my life, I was routinely and increasingly sucked into a way of living that was firmly on the Devil's terms. Although I'd never really set out purposely to do the wrong thing, I'd allowed myself to be seduced by worldly values and the pursuit of getting close to the people I was supposed to save. I'd been too weak and out of control to see through the craving to gain some sort of approval from them.

Perhaps the real point was this: What if God had come to earth and discovered me on a night like that one? What if He judged my state of compromise and shame then, as indicative my worth to Him? Would He even contemplate allowing me a place in heaven? These are questions that I have asked myself frequently since.

That night was seeded with one final twist that would ensure these thoughts would also be on my mind the following morning.

For the most part, things passed me by from that point onwards. I inexplicably ordered more drinks and intermittently tried to talk to people in an effort to rebuild my credibility. But whenever I did, I seemed to be shunned or pushed to the sidelines as if they were irritated by me even being around. Ultimately I became resigned to watching things unfold from a distance, as if I was trapped behind a screen as everyone else got on with the night.

After a while, I finally acknowledged the futility of my quest and staggered despondently out of the bar alone.

Whereas the city had looked so colourful and inviting before, the reflection of street lights stretching gloomily across the pavement seemed to expose its loneliness now, and a rain shower was washing away any optimism that remained. I remember heading towards the bottom end of town to where the taxi rank was based. It was there – just a hundred yards or so from where other sad looking figures filed into the hackney carriages, I heard my name called across the night.

"Ed, is that you? Ed...Ed, over here."

I was aware that members of my parents' church would often visit Coventry city centre on the weekend, in order to undertake what they broadly described as 'community mission work.' What I could not have anticipated was for any of them to migrate across to Birmingham to do a similar thing there. But among a group of around six others, I soon tallied the vaguely familiar voice shouting at me with a figure across the street, and realized it belonged to Trudy from the youth group.

For the relatively brief period I had known her, Trudy had always taken a special interest in me. Back at the time when I would attend the group, it was as if she would try to talk to me on a more adult level, often making a point of asking me about my studies or for recommendations of films to watch. Even at the end of my time there, it was as if she believed my involvement with them could be rescued, despite others perhaps sensing my separation was more inevitable. Although I had not seen much of her for the last five or so years, she did not hesitate in greeting me with a smile of someone who genuinely considered themselves a friend.

I panicked. It was the sense of regret and shame that a young boy found stealing from a sister's money box or running away from home, might feel. What would she think of me now – like this?

She wasn't there to preach. Along with the others, her task was not necessarily even to talk about God. Their approach was much more about simply reaching out to those within the city who seemed lost, vulnerable, or upset. Tonight I probably qualified for all these categories, but the last thing I felt I needed was to be discovered or helped. I wanted to pretend I had not even seen or heard her, and as if to signal this, I stumbled backwards - overwhelmed by the speed at which Trudy bounded across the street towards me.

"Hello you. How are you doing?" she said.

Almost as quickly as the words emerged, she retreated — perhaps suddenly sensing how awkward I found bumping into her like this, or now realizing just how wasted I was. Like the hundreds of other drunks they would come across on such nights, her experience immediately shouted at her to be weary of me.

"It's good to see you," she said — a statement that only a second earlier had been completely true. "You're on your way home? You're okay? Do you have money for a taxi?"

The fresh air had done nothing to sober me up, and I could only mumble something painfully incoherent in response.

Now that I was confronted like this, I felt a pang of shame inside of me. I wanted to explain that this wasn't normal. I wanted somehow to convince her that I was actually one of *them*. But I knew I could not make my case with any articulacy.

And because of this, my only option was to get away from there as quickly as possible.

"I've got to go," I said, almost whispering.

And with that I turned, pulled the hood on my jacket over my head, and walked hurriedly away.

Trudy's face was the theme of what seemed like a dozen anxiety filled dreams the next morning. I woke up feeling like I might have missed an appointment with one of God's angels, and that nagging sense of regret would long outlast the physical sickness brought about by my inevitable hangover.

Of course, I realize now that the face I should have been focusing my thoughts upon was the one that had stared back up at me from the toilet bowl earlier on that evening. In a strange way, perhaps part of the reason I left Trudy without trying to explain my situation, was because now more than ever, I *was* becoming that drunken guy who stood before her. It was that same sense of my worldly self consuming me, that I had begun to contend with back at college.

Jesus made it clear that we could not conveniently divorce ourselves from our behaviour in the way I had been allowing myself to believe. We are all known by our actions.

"For a good tree does not bear bad fruit, nor does a bad tree bear good fruit" (Luke 6:43-44).

I would recover. In a few days, I'd overcome the feelings of disappointment and guilt and put myself before God to ask for forgiveness again. But this would not be the last time I would drop down so low. Typically, as the thought of such evenings ebbed away, so too did the urgency to question the dangerous direction my life was taking.

Of course deep down, I knew that all was far from well with my plan. Although I was still trying hard not to acknowledge it, I was perhaps further than ever from doing God's work.

Avoiding the trap I had fallen into was not necessarily about keeping away from pubs or nightclubs, or even alcohol altogether. Like it or not, young people will socialize at such places, and in any case, I could not really blame what had happened upon where I was, or who I was with that night, despite the drinking games. It was much more about the strength of my own convictions and how I had unconsciously begun to switch my Christian life on and off as it suited me.

To that end perhaps the thought of what God's reaction would have been had he descended unexpectedly upon earth, was a useful and sobering question for me during that period. Sometimes it's easy to forget *He is* always there, witnessing the ugliest things we do and defying Him. He sees all this and still goes on loving us.

But at this time, I was more afraid to look into the face of my Father, just in case I caught a glimpse of His disappointment. I just did not feel like I was worthy of this most precious love. And this increasingly led me to look elsewhere for approval and acceptance.

Closet Christian

Sadly, things can get so bad that even when you do talk to God, alone - where no one else will see or hear, you sound like an animal moaning. You ask repeatedly for Him to make things better. You are scared of what the Devil might do, knowing that you have lived so often on his terms.

More and more you feel suffocated by the person you have been pretending to be. When you open your mouth that person seems to speak. He follows you around like a stench you can't wash away. At certain moments, you are desperate to rid yourself of him.

But, this is the shame of it – you often secretly hope that God doesn't do anything significant to shake him off. The Monday to Sunday that you have constructed – a week that is almost identical to that of a non-believer – feels strangely safe now. It's been so long that the thought of what He might do to challenge and disrupt your life, is almost as worrying as the prospect of never rediscovering the old you.

And when this happens, you know things have gotten pretty bad. When you simply don't trust what comes out of your mouth anymore – not even when those words are said to Him – that's when you know you have spent too long just following the noise of the crowd.

That's when you have to admit you're lost and face up to the reality of what you have become.

That's when you are the closet Christian.

But it can take some time to arrive at the point where you are prepared to admit this. It took me years.

It was over two days at work, when this became most apparent.

I had begun that particular week in a fairly restless and determined mood, convincing myself that I should not let it slip by without doing something of note - something different. I felt the need to reconnect to my old life, and speaking to David or Sam seemed like a good first step.

Although I always considered our friendship as unbreakable, there were still long periods when I had little or no contact with either of them. Our lives frequently branched off in separate directions, and to my dismay, this time two years had somehow passed since we had shared so much as a phone call.

It was natural for me to look towards them now. I associated them with the times that I had felt happiest and closest to God. I was intrigued to know what they were doing and daydreamed about us re-initiating the group together, or even finding our way back to Hathernwray.

But Thursday had come around before I knew it, and I still hadn't made the call. It had seemed like a busy week, but I couldn't put my finger on why. At this point, I tried not to analyse things too closely, probably knowing the layers of routine and ritual that I would find if I did.

I didn't need remarkable things to happen to appreciate that I needed a fresh start. It was at peculiar moments - tightening the knot on my tie in the mirror, putting my key in the ignition to start the car or perhaps kicking my shoes off at the end of the day - when I would suddenly get a strange sensation, like I was trapped on a roundabout, revolving to the same point over and over again. I wasn't achieving anything, just beating out the path of least resistance, and as my days filed by, I became more jaded and more cynical.

And born out of that cynicism, darker and more problematic thoughts had begun flashing across my mind recently – thoughts that went to the heart of my Christianity. I didn't doubt the existence of God or the part He had played in my life, but sometimes, for a split second, the apparent irrationality of it all stopped me in my tracks. What would I do if it *was* all an illusion? It was as if all my years of inactivity as a Christian had left gaps in my faith's defence.

As I walked from my car towards the office that day, I promised myself that I would contact Sam or David before the weekend. But right now, I was just focused on getting to that point without being hampered or tripped up by anything that might crop up at work. I had a habit of expecting things to go wrong there, and sometimes they did.

"You're here. Bernie wants to see us in his office in fifteen minutes."

It was around eighteen months since *that night* in Birmingham when I had embarrassed myself so emphatically in front of Jude and my other work colleagues. Presuming that she had formed a rather low opinion of me as a result, I had largely avoided her in the time since, and our only conversations had followed accidental meetings as we queued in the canteen or at the photocopier. There weren't too many elements at our jobs, which meant that our paths would cross. But now she was the one saying that Bernie needed to see *us*. I struggled to think of a reason for him to get us together, and given my frame of mind, assumed it must be bad news.

Bernie was the general manager and owner of the marketing agency. Having started out as a designer, he had built the business up from scratch – something he reminded us of most days. Such was his own devotion to it, he blindly assumed that everyone else who worked there shared the sense of dedication to each account that he had, and he often looked surprised, even offended, when you stood up to go home at night, no matter what the time was.

He was short but stocky, with a shaven head and neck that seemed as thick as the base of an old tree. Most people who had worked there a reasonable amount of time agreed that he was actually 'okay - once you got to know him,' but his slightly demanding style, physique and habitually cross facial expression, created a tough overall demeanour.

As we approached his office, Jude and I would quickly discover that his mood on this occasion was far more irritable than even his reputation suggested. We were still several feet down the corridor when the sound of the bin crashing to the floor — presumably having been kicked — and Bernie cursing, reached us.

"Eight years," he said to us as we walked in, as if we should automatically understand the statement.

One of the designers had already arrived, and was looking pensively on.

"We have had the Midlander's Choice account for eight years," Bernie continued, "and now — *now* they ask us to pitch for our *own* business. Can you believe it? I've known Ron down there for years. Haven't we always delivered?"

This was bad.

"Well, we'll give them a bloody pitch. If that's what Ron wants, that's what he'll get. That's what *you* lot are going to deliver."

This was really bad. Midlander's Choice was a local producer of frozen foods such as pies and pasties, and one of only a handful of regular clients that the agency had managed to retain. As Bernie had mentioned, he and the Managing Director of Midlander's Choice went back a long way. Having set-out supplying local stores and corner shops, they had grown rapidly, to the point that they now supplied their products through supermarkets across the country. But there were rumours that business had not been so good in recent months. Despite what Bernie was saying, the last series of adverts that we had placed for them had not generated anything like the response that previous campaigns had.

"Jude, I know this is out of scope for you, but I need someone I can trust to manage this. We have to present concepts to them first thing Monday morning. Dom, you are our creative lead — they're looking for press advertising. Ed, you support them with whatever they need."

I nodded, feeling underwhelmed by my role, and having been made uncomfortable by the urgency of the situation.

It was the sort of situation I loathed. It wasn't that I was ineffective at work - I tried hard and my contribution was well appreciated. I also wanted to do well.

But if I was honest, I was more focused on doing everything I could to not mess up rather than making a real name for myself. I sensed that Bernie saw me as solid and reliable rather than one of his high flyers.

I liked to do things at my own speed. I've reflected since, that my working style is probably similar to that of a clock repairer — methodically and painstakingly taking the different devices apart, before fixing them and putting them back together. Certainly, I didn't feel that I performed well in a crisis, and always hoped that the weeks would ebb away inconsequentially rather than end with any sort of crescendo.

I had earmarked that day for reading through a couple of briefs we had received, sending a few unimportant e-mails, and putting the finishing touches to a report I had been writing. Bernie had other ideas:

"Clear your diaries people, and be prepared to work late. This is your chance to impress."

The rest of the day was spent, idea generating, strategy planning, analysing the market, prioritising our tactics, and most of all, trying to figure out what might make people buy more Midlander's Choice' frozen food. We worked frenetically around the large boardroom table like bees busily extracting the pollen from a flower. Every now and then one of us would dart from our seats towards the wall to record more of the output from our session on a large whiteboard, or add another handful of *Post-It* note ideas to those already stuck-up, before heading back.

Jude led the process with the ruthlessness and determination that Bernie had expected. We didn't really stop. If Dom or I momentarily lost focus, or just for some respite, began joking, she would instantly remind us of the job in hand.

"Come on guys, stay with it," she said while tapping her watch to remind us of the tight deadline.

It was estimable and infuriating at the same time.

Inevitably there were periods when our progress was less tangible than others, but by the time Bernie came to check on us at about five-thirty, we had come up with the outline to three separate campaign options. Of course, he wanted to understand each one in great detail – to think how they might be received by Ron at Midlander's Choice. Another hour had passed before he was satisfied enough to leave us and go home, promising that he would tell us his preference the following day.

Home was where I wanted to go too. Jude had other ideas.

"Guys, you've worked hard, how about I treat you to dinner?"

I knew straight away that her motivation wasn't to reward us for what we had done so far, but to coax out even more from us. Jude was a smart operator, but quickly realized that we would see through her barely disguised plan.

"It will give us a chance to get ahead of ourselves – take the pressure off for tomorrow," she added, more honestly now.

As soon as Dom reluctantly nodded his head to agree, I had little option but to go along with it as well. We headed for the local pub.

Unfortunately our day, which until this point had been relatively productive, was destined to take a turn for the worse. Our work continued when we got there, but with less output and less harmony than before. The food we ordered took a long time to arrive and the combination of hunger and tiredness seemed to make us increasingly irritable.

It started with Dom and Jude disagreeing about which of the three options we should present to Midlander's Choice. Dom preferred a campaign based around a straightforward offer of 'Three for Two' on their products, whereas Jude wanted to go with the option that focused on the quality and taste of the food as the main selling point.

Without really having a strong opinion either way, I soon found myself silently rooting for Dom. As June went on, she seemed so stubborn and obstinate that I began to find her irritating.

"No sorry Dom, I can't see it. I know the 'Three-For-Two' offer has worked in the past, but it will mean less margin for Midlander's Choice, and I think we are going to have problems selling that to Ron right now. Let's go with the 'taste' option."

I reflected again on the only other time I'd really seen her out of work, and struggled to understand why I had been so desperate to impress her back then.

"Besides, your work on the 'taste' option is excellent. Dom, I really have to say that it is some of your best work," she said.

She was obviously trying to manipulate Dom again and I'd had enough. I knew that I couldn't bear much more.

"Jude, have you actually tasted a Midlander's Choice pie recently?"

She looked at me as if I had made the most absurd and irrelevant statement that she had ever heard.

I was unperturbed.

"Well I have, and they're disgusting – they're vile. So what's the point in trying to pretend anything else?"

These were unusually antagonistic comments for me and probably unnecessary. Jude put me in my place.

"Edward please," she came back immediately, "it doesn't matter what they actually taste like. If we can create the impression of people enjoying them, then people *will* convince themselves they like the taste."

What Jude had said seemed nonsensical – spurious – and undermining. And that seemingly beguiling logic wasn't the last that I would encounter that night.

It was past eleven by the time I got back to my flat. I was exhausted, but could not face going straight to bed, especially with so many elements of what we had been discussing earlier swilling around my head.

I decided to watch some television to unwind. From the comfort of my sofa, I pressed the 'on' button on my remote control and watched the light rupture from the middle of the screen before spreading out to form the picture. Feeling too drained to even discern between what was on the different channels, I sat back, prepared to absorb whatever program happened to appear before me.

This scheduling lottery served up a documentary about a group of neuroscientists in Austria. Led by a guy named Professor Holzknecht at the Hoffnung Institute, their research focused on the biological activity of the mind during periods of significant emotion such as 'happiness' or 'grief,' and whether these patterns could be artificially stimulated. Specifically, they were building computerized models to simulate the process of transmitting small electrical pulses through different areas of the brain.

I am pretty sure that I dropped off to sleep for large portions of the program as I didn't really follow how much progress they had actually made. I did though, take in enough detail to realize that they had attracted significant criticism and controversy. Aside from the more obvious moral questions regarding their techniques, they made no secret of their ultimate objective of transferring this work into actual human practice, with a view to commercializing their services. Towards its conclusion, and at a point I was following more consciously again, the program's commentator chillingly observed:

'In the strange world of Professor Holzknecht and his colleagues 'Happiness,' 'Optimism,' even 'Love' might one day be products that customers could choose from a catalogue of emotions. Their work continues, seemingly with little regard for the intellectual and ethical debate that ensues, but questions remain: How can science ever anticipate or guard against the broader psychological impact this type of interference could have? What guarantees are there that these practices will be used responsibly?'

I was tired – too tired to really evaluate the authenticity of it all. But even so, there seemed something sinister in what I had been watching. I was still awake, but at the point where your brain conveniently rearranges the boundaries of your life in an attempt to make logic of the day's events. In this state of semiconsciousness, Jude's incomprehensible opinion that we could convince people to like Midlander's Choice food despite the taste, and Professor Holzknecht's dubious scientific objectives, became part of the same conundrum. They were both threats to truth and reason. As I sat there in the dark, my ability to hold onto anything as being incontestably true, felt like it was being undermined.

The next time I opened my eyes, two Sumo wrestlers converged from either side of the television screen before slamming their huge flabby bodies against each other. I realized I must have dozed-off again. My sleep so far had been troubled and I was sweating.

Still not bothering to undress, the last thing I remember was switching off the television and stumbling over to my bed, determined to think about something less taxing.

In many ways my response to these things were predictable and traceable to my broader crisis. During this period of my life, anything that hinted at gaps in how I rationalized, seemed to amplify my insecurities about what I actually believed. Though I tried to resist the realization, so much of what I read or watched was prone to chip away at my faith.

I was starting to judge Christianity as something more fallible than before. I even began to consider how easily Jesus' message could have been diluted and changed as it was passed down to me through time. What if I didn't really understand God or what He wanted? What about all the other religions in the world? Was it arrogant to dismiss them as simply wrong or untrue? It would be some time before I could satisfy myself over these things.

Professor Holzknecht and Jude were still on my mind as I apathetically prodded the cereal in my bowl the following morning - not really feeling hungry enough to eat. But by now, I was slightly less disturbed by them. The pragmatism of getting ready for work somehow made my anxieties seem less imminent.

I felt more at ease for at least having started to understand the root cause of my concerns. At times like this, I was sure 'better' Christians would simply dip into the reserves of faith they had built up from countless church sermons and hours of prayer, but I had let my stocks run worryingly low.

It was a logic that I allowed myself to develop as I rode the bus into town. I was still in the habit of leaving the car at home on Fridays just in case we headed out for a drink after work, even if this happened less frequently now. As I'd sat down, I had instinctively reached for a book in my bag, but before even opening it to start reading, I had begun to reflect more broadly. Perhaps I *was* just missing the fellowship that had been such a blessing at Hathernwray. I needed someone to provide the counterbalance to my doubts — whatever this was.

I realized then, that I hadn't had a chance to call David or Sam again the previous evening. Despite the Midlander's Choice work, the day had been typical of how I'd let myself become trapped and inactive. There was always something getting in the way. If it wasn't a pitch to hurriedly prepare, then there was something else distracting me from the life I wanted to lead.

I pushed the bell to indicate to the driver that I wanted the next stop. I would soon be at work, but I promised myself I would make *that* call - very soon.

Having believed things were under control with the pitch, later that morning we would find ourselves up against the clock once again. Bernie informed us that he didn't particularly like the 'Taste' campaign which Jude had favoured, or the 'Three-for-Two' option. Instead, he preferred our third approach which tried to promote the brand as the family choice of convenience foods, and insisted it was this one we should take back to the client.

Unfortunately, by the time the verdict was delivered, we had already spent the first two hours of the day busily preparing the first of these, given that Jude had convinced us that this would definitely be Bernie's choice as well.

Dom specifically faced an uphill task in getting the concept boards completed in time. In fact, while Jude and I could contribute in a fairly minor way by preparing our supporting documents, most of the work would now fall to him.

Edward's Choice

The burden weighed heavily upon him for most of the morning. He stared intensely at his computer monitor, almost as if allowing his eyes to wander would mean that his momentum would be lost irretrievably. His mouse moved around frantically, like he was busily fixing errors that were spontaneously appearing about his work across the screen. Jude and I would hardly dare to talk to him.

And yet, with such clarity around our roles and the fast approaching deadline, the disagreements and bickering of the previous evening stopped. Jude in particular was going out of her way to demonstrate her humility and sense of regret for what had happened. She kept Dom constantly stocked with a supply of coffee and pastries, and humbly went about completing some of the less glamorous tasks like typing up our notes and proof reading our documents. Whether he had intended it or not (and he probably hadn't), by over-ruling all of us with his choice of approach, Bernie had reunited our group and ensured any residual annoyance would be turned upon him.

This pressure would last for most of the day, and only at about four o'clock did the sense of concern begin to lift and the mood lightened. While it was clear that there was still much to do, at this point Dom suddenly seemed to loosen up - relaxing back into his chair and smiling knowingly, as if to say that he was now confident everything was under control. Jude and I took our lead from him.

Indeed a little later, as Bernie practised the presentation he would give, the atmosphere between the three of us became almost triumphant, like the sense of relief you experience when you walk out of the room at the end of an examination. Still listening to Bernie rehearse, Jude leaned over and whispered in my ear.

"I suppose you're right."

I looked around at her, with what must have been a confused look on my face, making clear I hadn't grasped her meaning.

"You were right about Midlander's Choice pies," she explained, "they probably are revolting."

"We're done. How about a drink to celebrate?" said Dom later, once Bernie had declared himself satisfied enough to leave.

"Absolutely," Jude responded.

"I don't know about you two, but right now I really couldn't care less what Ron thinks on Monday. We've done our bit."

Whether she was being completely honest in this declaration or not, there was no sense of an ulterior motive in her joining us now.

My ambition to make this week notable – to make some sort of change, had never been far from my mind, but I knew that I would go along with their suggestion, even though it would sideline my plan to call Sam or David for at least another day. I rapidly gathered my bag and jacket and followed the others.

What I couldn't have expected, as I left the building, was that the city itself could provide the impetus I was looking for; that *it* could play a role in my steady reawakening.

We bypassed those bars we typically visited with other colleagues from work. In some small way we seemed to have bonded as a team now, and I for one was glad that there would be no opportunity for someone like Tony to muscle in on our night.

The main square was predictably busy. It was early evening and a peak period when the shoppers and office workers who were still making their way home, briefly mixed with the first of the night's revellers and diners. Rather than the chaos and hurrying around that was typical of the morning rush hour though, tonight it all added to a relaxed and expectant atmosphere.

The noise was a wonderful part of it all. It came from a combination of sources: music escaping from the bars and pubs, buskers playing their guitars, people nattering, and market traders croaking desperately into the evening to sell the last of their goods. They came together to create a rich auditory portrait of the city, and I felt oddly satisfied to be there. It was a subtly pleasurable few moments that everyone seemed invited to join.

But something else would wrestle away our attention relatively quickly. As we walked to the far side of the square, I gradually became aware of music of a different kind. From an old building now renovated as a meeting venue, the sound of instruments playing and people singing echoed out onto the road and began to build in our collective consciousness.

I soon realized that this was music I recognized. But it was more than that. It was something more personal to me. It was a hymn. After a few seconds I realized that the song I was listening to, was *Shine Jesus Shine.*

This was so unexpected and out of context that I was taken aback. Encountering this in these surroundings was like one of the most personal moments of my life being suddenly broadcast across a public address system.

For some reason, I felt that my connection to it must be obvious to the others. But looking up, it was unlikely that anyone had even noticed my reaction. Instead the throng of faces about me were all staring towards the building where it was coming from, even though there was nothing really visible to reveal what was going on inside.

Amazingly, they were drawn to the music themselves. People were getting into what they heard – liking it. Some hummed along, and a line of girls who stood on the town hall steps close by bent their knees and clapped as if they might be at a pop concert. There was no distinction about who seemed to be getting involved. Without exception, it spontaneously painted smiles on the faces of businessmen and women, people carrying shopping bags, as well as those, who like us, had stopped on their way to the various bars and pubs. Even a gang of youths who only a few moments before had been crisscrossing the square on skateboards, stopped for a few moments to join the audience – giving each other 'high fives' to signal their unlikely approval.

It was strange. I'd spent so much time recently contemplating how outdated and implausible my Christian beliefs were being made to feel in this world. But here today – this music, and this worship, had somehow become such a fresh and real part of society again. Right now it was the heartbeat of the city.

Jonathan Young

As soon as I had overcome my unnecessary self-consciousness, I allowed myself to reflect personally on what I was hearing. On one level, it seemed like a sweet reminder to me - a homing device calling me back to where I belonged. But at the same time it made me feel uncomfortable — saddened even. I was so far removed from it.

Deep down I wished I could follow the music into that building. I wanted what the people inside had — their fellowship. But I wouldn't do anything about it. In fact, I didn't even bother to pose myself the question, knowing that the thought of how Jude and Dom might react would paralyse me. And acknowledging this, my situation instantly seemed so much more desperate than it had before. The taste of what I'd been missing was on my lips, but was still inaccessible to me, and I had bluntly confirmed to myself that I was worthless to God right now.

For that reason, I went from enjoying the music to wanting it to stop. It was perhaps at that moment more than any other when I realized something *would* have to change, but there and then, I felt powerless.

Eventually, it was Dom who broke the spell.

"What about that? Amazing eh? Let's get that drink."

We did as he suggested.

Strangely, other than that, none of us would really discuss what we had experienced there on the square during the rest of that night, and I was relieved. I felt like I needed time to gather my thoughts.

When you live like this — locking your Christianity away in a room, creeping back only sporadically to pacify yourself with a few mechanical words of prayer - its just a matter of time before the thing you locked away starts to seem strange or alien to you. The voices on the outside fill your head with doubt - decrying what you believe as just another story or fable that mankind has created for his own self-serving purposes. Before you know it, your relationship with God can begin to feel like an awkward little secret.

Because of all those years of lies, this is where I had ended up. Although I'd been pretending to do His work, I'd actually been listening to those voices for so long now I could not ignore their clamour to somehow prove His existence in my life.

Of course, the Bible makes it clear that those in need of such proof are merely confirming their own inability to truly see, as when those who passed Jesus on the cross, taunted Him and dared Him to save Himself (Mark 15:29-32; Matthew 27:39-42). Indeed from when He was sentenced to be crucified by Pontius Pilate (Luke 23:13-25), to when His resurrection was concealed (Matthew 28:11), Jesus' life demonstrated the fallibility of man's own filters of truth and logic and how these would be manipulated.

What I needed was the faith to see again – faith that I had lost by believing a Christian Life could be somehow lived undercover or in secret.

I was lost, cut adrift, but things would get better. As uncomfortable as those moments had been when the sound of worship echoed out across the city centre that day, their unsettling affect upon me was an indication that my own senses were returning.

Contact

"*Hi, this is David's phone. I'm not available to take your call right now, but leave a message and I'll get back to you.*"

I hung up, too proud to leave another message, and resigned to the fact that I wouldn't press redial again. I'd been trying to contact David for about a week without any success. It was the same with Sam. It was strange. I assumed that they simply weren't around, or just didn't want to talk to me. There was no obvious explanation for either scenario, but having spent so long knowingly shunning the reality of what was happening in my life, I was less convinced of my ability to read situations correctly these days.

Any Christian will tell you, that living a Christian life isn't always straightforward. As my own situation had shown, there can be dark moments when you feel alone – abandoned even – when the pleas for help you make just don't feel like they have the wings to make it to Him. It can be especially frustrating when you think you know exactly the help you need. From asking for His guidance, you begin expecting Him to implement the future you have envisaged. It is easy to forget that God is the only one who ever truly sees the plot in advance.

I've often slipped into the habit of trying to anticipate how my prayers would be answered.

This was the situation I found myself in as I waited for some sort of deliverance.

In many ways, this was my most testing time. I felt in limbo. Having dropped down so low and finally mustered the courage to seek help, I'd perhaps assumed that it would arrive straight away – afraid that the scrap of faith that I had rediscovered might not sustain me for much longer.

Happily, I would not have to wait too long. It was the week before Christmas.

It was possibly because of the advancing festivities that I felt the right to be optimistic. Although I was unlikely to admit it to anyone, privately I believed that there was something very special about Christmas - something that could make the happy endings played-out in the films and television shows at this time of year, somehow transfer across into real life.

I had, what I thought were fairly traditional Christmas values - though looking back they were more a strange mix of themes and customs that were significant only for having survived in my memory from childhood. The way I'd grown to cherish the Nativity story was an example of this. Of course, I'd heard the biblical accounts of this at Sunday school and would have noticed it depicted on Christmas cards and other decorations, but most of all, this passion was fuelled by recollections of an ornamental nativity scene that my parents would put out each year when I was young. I'd spend time just looking into it from different positions, as if the light shining across the figurines within told a new story with each angle. To me, that cattle shed was the most cosy and harmonious place imaginable. Perhaps oddly, I'd even daydreamed about being one of them – an unreported onlooker towards the back, just lying against the hay and sharing the miracle.

But my notions of what Christmas should be were not all around Christian theme – far from it. Sure I loved Christmas carols, but songs like *The Christmas Song* sung by Bing Crosby or David Essex's version of *A Winter's Tale* were just as much a part of it all for me. I would also eagerly sit down with the *Radio Times* each year to pick those television highlights that I knew would stir my enthusiasm for the festive period: an eclectic and often childish selection that included things like *The Snowman* and *Miracle on 34th Street,* as well as Christmas specials for comedies like *The Vicar of Dibley*. Christmas was this and so many other things – exchanging cards, visiting those streets that were renowned for outlandishly lit up houses, eating an extraordinarily large Christmas dinner – and if any of these things were missing then it just wasn't the same.

The problem was, that I wanted to experience all this from a foundation of broader contentment. My life didn't have to be perfect, but I at least needed signs that it could get better - hope to ease me into the New Year. Without this, the arrival of these emblems of Christmas could start to feel slightly uncomfortable and wasted.

Nothing that had happened this year had punctured my romantic aspirations for Christmas, but as I forlornly slipped my phone into my pocket having tried to ring David, I was beginning to worry that it might all just pass me by. I hadn't wanted things to hinge on *them*, but more and more they felt like gatekeepers to the festive period I wanted.

I'd made the call, stood in the long queue to the cash machine just outside Birmingham's main shopping centre. I was in town to start my Christmas shopping, but having unwisely set about the task without any particular ideas for presents, I was already feeling slightly frustrated and beaten. Whereas I had been walking aimlessly in and out of stores, other shoppers seemed to have more purpose, and highlighted my own ineffectiveness with the number of shopping bags they had already collected.

It was also raining – heavily. I could feel the water permeating uncomfortably through the fabric of my suit trousers and jacket and sticking my shirt to my torso like a scaly second skin.

For some reason it seemed like these and other afflictions were inviting me to feel sorry for myself. But I would not let it happen. I was determined to resist self-pity and at least preserve the idea that Christmas might come good for me. I decided that I would try my luck in just one or two more shops before heading home.

On my walk up to the car park, I was made to weave in and out of several clusters of bodies as they filed along the pavement between the pubs and hotels. The atypical mix of relatively young and older-looking people - those who seemed to be in familiar surroundings and others who looked slightly embarrassed to be there, perhaps suggested that they were out on office Christmas parties, rather than being regular social companions. By now it was the Thursday before Christmas and the most popular period for these events.

I became aware of one such group when I almost collided with two guys as they staggered out of a hotel lobby and onto the street in front of me. They were about my age, and like me, they were wearing business suits, but had ties that were loosened to hang untidily around their necks. One of them briefly paused and looked around as if to concede his part in our near-accident, but quickly turned away again, throwing his arm around his friend's neck and shouting out a football-style chant to no-one in particular.

Anticipating that they might be the first in another tide of merrymakers, I decided to hang back, leaving room for them to exit before attempting to walk past the hotel doors.

It proved to be a wise move. A man and women, who looked far more conservative, came out soon after. In contrast, they were talking more intently, as if they might be discussing an important issue from work, like an invoice they had just remembered needed paying. They revealed their connection to the first two men only with a begrudging nod in their direction, and hung around for a few seconds – tampering with an umbrella, as if to let a safe distance between them develop.

The remainder of their party emerged almost immediately – this time in one large rowdy group. The majority of them were girls, wearing short evening dresses and high heels that made them walk with large ungraceful steps -'click-clacking' like horses kicking their hooves on the pavement below. Despite them creating a fairly intimidating racket, there was something in their rawness that made them instantly likeable.

If one of them exemplified this more than any other, it was a plump and bubbly girl who seemed to bound person to person as if there were too many bodies on offer to dedicate herself to anyone completely. I noticed that she wore tinsel in her hair, and was brashly carrying around a piece of mistletoe, as if to advertise the fact she was looking for a man with whom to share some 'Christmas cheer.'

And after a few seconds of being out on the street, it became clear she had identified a possible target. She called forward in the direction of the guy who had earlier been fiddling with the umbrella - walking down the hotel steps towards him at the same time.

"Warren, how about a Christmas kiss?"

He turned back, perhaps unwisely acknowledging that he'd heard. Realizing that she was heading in his direction, his expression changed from one of surprise to a slightly pained smile, and then to a much more alarmed look, all within a few moments. Her advances obviously wouldn't be reciprocated, and he evidently wouldn't hang around to see just how persistent she might be either. Moving as quickly as she had, he abandoned his colleague and jogged forward for a few footsteps, apparently finding the prospect of catching up with his more boisterous workmates in front more desirable now.

"Oh Warrren," she repeated, in a disappointed faltering tone, "it's only a kiss - where's your Christmas spirit?"

By now she stood almost parallel to where I was still waiting. I momentarily panicked that she had identified me as her next victim, but it was an unjustified concern. She turned around to me, broke into a large resigned grin and shrugged her shoulders.

"Miserable. Well you can't blame a girl for trying can you? Merry Christmas."

"Merry Christmas," I replied.

She rejoined the rest of the group as they marched away to continue their evening.

Clearly I wasn't the only one who was feeling slightly spurned and disappointed this Christmas period. I smiled to myself, hoping that God would somehow come to the aid of all those who needed a lift at this time – whatever the context. Especially those, who despite the most trying circumstances, were still finding reason to be positive.

And so I spent the next few days getting ready for Christmas - while also waiting. *What* I was waiting for was less clear. Maybe a sign? A phone call? All I knew was that I had to believe things could get better, because in my prayers I asked that they would. Yet with each day that passed, that expectation perhaps diminished a fraction more.

But then hope did arrive. Indeed, with the sort of ironic punch-line that such frustrating situations often deliver, my quest to contact David and Sam would eventually be answered by not one of the guys, but both, within a short space of time.

It was Christmas Eve and I had driven back to Coventry soon after breakfast, having finished work the day before. When I arrived at my parent's house it seemed uncharacteristically quiet, and it was only having let myself in and discarded my bags, that I discovered my dad sitting alone lounging in front of the television.

Without really turning to focus on me, he mumbled something about my mom having gone out to deliver some Christmas cards and there being food in the fridge if I wanted a snack, before re-immersing himself in the program that he was watching. He clearly wasn't much in the mood for conversation, and I had no particular reason to interrupt, so I decided to go upstairs to kill some time catching up with e-mails on my parents' computer.

There in amongst ten or so lines of unread notes I spotted the correspondence from David Stone. I could barely move the cursor over it rapidly enough.

Hey Ed,

How's your Christmas so far? Sorry not to have been in touch (I know you've heard it all before), but this time my excuse is pretty good.

I'm writing this from BRAZIL. No I'm not joking. I've been over here for three weeks doing some work – but I'm heading back. I'm actually in Sao Paulo airport waiting for my flight right now.

Mate, it's been amazing – mind blowing. Can't wait to tell you more and find out what you've been up to.

I'll call you when I'm back and settled after Christmas.

Have a great one. D.

Straight away, I glanced back over the e-mail, eager to check on what I thought I'd read. It was so full of intrigue and promise. I instantly felt encouraged by the situation he had found himself in, as if it was proof that wonderful, amazing changes could actually happen in people's lives – that they might happen in mine. The line, *'I'll call you when I'm back and settled after Christmas'* seemed like a contract to involve me in it all.

I was still taking it all in when I heard my mom calling up from downstairs.

Edward's Choice

"Edward honey, we're back. You okay? Did Dad mention there was food if you wanted it?"

Having satisfied myself that I hadn't misjudged or even imagined anything the first time around, I switched off the computer. I was impatient to understand more, but already I was much more cheerful than before.

I was greeted in the Kitchen by a hug from my mom and sister. They were excited and pleased to see me, but I could see that they were also looking forward to my arrival for more practical reasons. A set of stepladders were propped ready against the wall and I was handed a box of decorations that had been intentionally set aside for me to hang from various elevated points around the walls and ceiling. I didn't mind. In fact, as if I had finally received my invite to share in the celebrations and festivities, I now felt in a hurry to embrace it all.

As I stood up there trying to unpick the end of the sticky tape from the roll to begin my work, my mom made me a sandwich while at the same time updating me about the latest from our friends and family.

"You never guess who we ran into today?" she said after a short time.

Of course I had no chance of knowing, and shrugged my shoulders somewhat indifferently.

"Sam Herring's mom."

I stopped what I was doing and looked down at her.

"Sam's mom?" I replied, in a tone that I hoped would urge her to speed up her story.

"Yeah — I was dropping off a few cards in church ahead of midnight mass tonight, and she happened to be doing the same thing. Did you know that Sam's been in a hospital for the last two weeks, poor boy?"

My stunned expression must have told her that I didn't.

"Hospital?"

I couldn't keep up. It was like she was throwing huge rocks into a pool that was still rippling from David's unexpected update.

"Apparently he's had some sort of chest infection, but I didn't like to pry too much. Sounds awful. Anyway, the good news is he's home for Christmas."

"I didn't know," I said almost apologetically – only now answering her initial question.

"I didn't think so. Oh well, his mom promised that she would get him to give you a call."

Sam ill? David in Brazil? It seemed so implausible - as if circumstance had pitched the guys in the most extreme scenarios possible to demonstrate just how out of touch with them I had become. I was naturally concerned about Sam and my head was spinning.

But despite this – and although I felt somewhat guilty for it – I was pleased for at least having had *some* news. To a large degree it was as if Christmas had been rescued because of these updates and the possibilities they created. Over the next few hours, as more members of the family arrived for our traditional Christmas Eve gathering, I found myself in a much better mood. In fact, from that point on, I was even happy to act as ringleader for much of the merriment: chatting enthusiastically with those I hadn't seen for a while, organising party games, and in the case of the children there, fuelling their excitement with talk of Santa Claus and presents.

Almost as if I'd had my worries temporarily lifted, I at last had moments of fun and laughter that didn't seem contaminated by an underlying sense of my dissatisfaction. I resisted trying to anticipate what David and Sam's update might mean. That could wait. For the time-being, I was happy to simply enjoy those hours without thinking about anything else.

Just as my mom had promised, it wasn't long before I'd hear from Sam. In fact, he rang on the afternoon of the following day - Christmas Day.

It was a reflection of just how well liked he was within my family, that of all the calls my mom picked up that day, *his* was the one that was most eagerly received. She had been worried for him, and frustratingly for me, spent several minutes telling him so before handing over the receiver.

As soon as our conversation began, I noticed how weak his voice sounded compared to before. He apologized for not having returned my calls.

"Forget it," I responded. "How are you now? What on earth has been going on?"

"Yeah I'm okay."

"Okay?" I said disbelievingly.

"It was nothing really."

"Nothing? They don't keep you in hospital for two weeks for nothing mate."

There was an uncomfortable pause on the line. Either he was just eager to forget his ordeal, which was very possible, or for some reason he felt awkward discussing it. Whichever, I decided that it was best to leave the subject alone, so began asking about David.

"What's all this about David in Brazil?"

"Unreal isn't it. You know he's normally so composed about everything, but *this* has really got to him – in a good way I mean. He went over with some of the guys from church. They've been setting up shelters for the homeless kids in the city over there."

I listened in silence to this and his explanation around how the trip had come about, but in truth my concentration had been trapped by one of the things he had uttered at the start.

"Church?" I asked somewhat desperately, when he had finished.

I knew that *our* youth group had come to end shortly after I had left for college, but for some reason it hadn't occurred to me that they could have found another place to go since, without me knowing.

"Yeah we met some guys from a church over in Rugby, and thought we'd give it a try. It's only been the last eighteen months or so," he began explaining quickly.

Sam obviously sensed that I felt slightly overlooked for not having been told.

"You should come along sometime - when David gets back I mean?" he said, clearly trying to amend for it.

It wasn't his fault. What right had I to expect anything from them giving our lack of contact in recent times? But at the same time it was still a way back – a chance that I didn't want to let pass.

"That would be great," I said.

Although our conversation had been short, he had begun to sound tired and out of breath.

"Listen mate, I'm knackered," he admitted, "I'll give you a call in a few days and we'll sort out you coming to Rugby with us?"

"Yeah absolutely, we'll do that."

"Have a great Christmas eh?" he said almost whispering now.

I heard the dialling tone return, so I hung up too.

I knew at the time, that this was God working in my life. It was almost certainly the case that if I'd gone on trying I would have tracked down David and Sam eventually, but the way it had happened suggested that these were His hands shaping my life again - twisting the dials on the future, to ensure my safe passage.

For that reason, it was a Christmas I'll always remember for being the start of better times for me. And yet, as the holiday period passed and my wonder at the sequence of events began to fade away, I'd run into familiar insecurities. Although I tried to ignore it, I couldn't help but feel slightly stung by the thought of David and Sam finding a new Christian fellowship without me. And now it was as if I was playing catch-up - piggy-backing on their lives.

I believe that God serves-up all manner of miracles every day, and that I've been a recipient of these on many occasions - interventions that have clearly answered my prayers. The problem is that you move on so quickly that those moments just tend to get filed away in your mind with all the other twists and turns that you encounter. Before you realize it, it's much more difficult to pick them out on the mixed landscape of your past.

Perhaps it is meant to be like this. Perhaps this is God's way of ensuring that we go on renewing our faith. Right now I had faith, and for the first time in awhile, I had more reason to look ahead than back into the past.

Alien

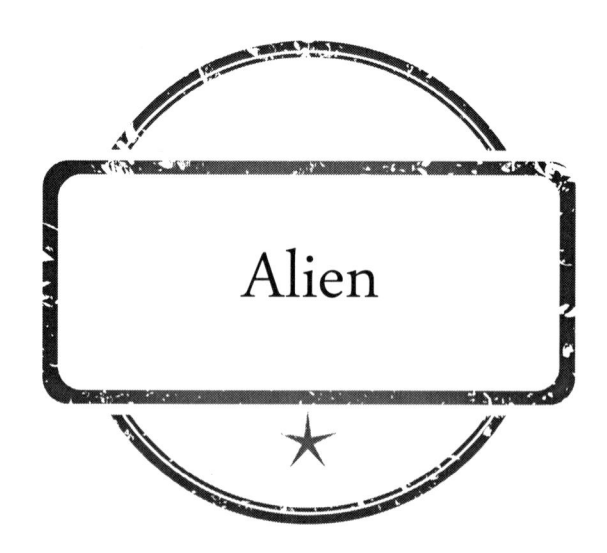

Over those years, I'd shut out 'the church' completely. My faith had become something entirely personal and even the idea of Christian fellowship felt slightly peculiar to me. I somehow had to find a way of easing myself back in again.

But who were the people who went to church?

It's probably the case that I've spent too much time worrying about other people, but in the days before going to the church in Rugby, it was a question that was occupying me a lot. I was desperate for the people there to accept me, and to have this happen I felt I needed to anticipate exactly who *they* were – how *they* had found their way there.

So like the clients of the advertising agency I worked for who would spend time profiling their customers based on how and why they bought their products, I began to think about churchgoers in a fairly formulaic way. And although it was a crude over-simplification, what I came up with was two categories of people that I thought I remembered from my old church group. There were those who had just always been around Christianity, from their families and their upbringing, and for whom attending church was just something they had always done. And then other individuals, whose journey there could be traced clearly back to significant events in their life - often turning to God through need or desperation following real sadness they had endured.

The fact that I fitted both of these norms to some degree wasn't lost on me. I was also aware though, that this wouldn't necessarily do anything to help my reintegration now. I couldn't escape the feeling that I would be somehow different. Even though David and Sam's presence there should have been testimony to the companionableness of the others that I might meet, it was as if I assumed my time away would have stained me in a way that would mark me out. It was on my mind a lot during those days.

If I've always loved Christmas, I've often found the period immediately afterwards to be a struggle. In many ways then, the start to that year was no different; like a fog descending around the fresh purpose and direction I'd discovered. During those first few mornings back, I woke up as if I'd been disturbed from hibernation rather than just one night's sleep, and I set out on my journey to work, feeling as fragile as the trees I saw being viciously bent over in the cold wind. More than ever, the long nights seemed to squeeze the life out of the days.

Work itself didn't offer any relief. During the early part of that week Bernie turned up in a particularly humourless mood, which in turn made the whole office uneasy. Although, there was no obvious peak in workload such as what we had experienced when preparing the Midlander's Choice pitch, he sighed audibly when walking past the empty desks of people who had taken extended breaks and muttered about how Christmas had 'left us behind.' The climax of this was when he made the receptionist cry by growling at her to take down a Christmas tree which stood belatedly in the foyer; as if *it* symbolised the legacy of last year's excesses.

I possibly had more reason than most to be alarmed by this phase of excessive sulkiness. On the Thursday evening I was due to attend the annual 'Fast Moving Consumer Goods Advertising Awards' ceremony – with *him*. To my surprise, a campaign for a brand of air-freshener that I had coordinated during the previous summer had been nominated in the 'Household and Domestic' category. Although Bernie was fairly dismissive about our chances of success, and was actually annoyed for not having been nominated for other work the agency had done, he had decided to 'reward' me by taking me along.

It was a happy distraction then, when David called-up unexpectedly to ask if he could come around the evening before this. He was still on a high from his trip and despite the years we'd allowed to go by since we were last together, clearly the weekend was too long to have to wait to tell me more about it now.

Having put down the phone, it seemed like no time at all before I heard the sound of his car pulling up outside my house, and soon I was rushing downstairs to open the door. More than ever, it felt like I was greeting a stranger as well as a friend.

"Have we got some catching up to do," he said immediately - perhaps not feeling the peculiarity of the situation in the way I was.

Everything about him, from his still tanned skin to his sunny enthusiasm, seemed to strike the most extreme contrast to the general dreariness that had arrived with the New Year in every other respect. There was a new confident aura about him somehow; one that made me feel fairly weak for the way I'd been tip-toeing through my days.

During the two hours or so he was there he did almost all the talking, while I mainly sat and listened. He had so much to share – so many stories to recount: the places he had visited; the vulnerability of the children they helped in Sao Paulo and Rio de Janeiro; the impact it was having. It flowed like a waterfall out of him.

I was struck by how much he spoke about God – casually and frequently referring to Him in the same way you might talk about a new friend that you were spending a lot of time with – but with real reverence.

"Ed, I can feel God telling me what to do now and His blessing follows," he said at one point.

I wasn't used to it. I wasn't even sure that I was ready for it. Although I tried not to, I was conscious that I impulsively broke eye contact with him each time he talked in this way, as if I was afraid he might look into my soul and see all the doubt that was in me.

Back at Hathernwray we were all witness to each other's gradual discovery of God, and at the time, there were a few poignant moments when we had acknowledged this to each other. But this seemed so long ago. It was as if Christianity was something David, Sam, and I recognized as a bond between us, but which we had since struck an understanding not to discuss. Now, consciously or not, he was changing the rules.

Not only that, *he* was changing. David was still the wise and likeable friend I've described, but in a good way his focus and forcefulness made him less comfortable to be with.

And the most notable thing he would say, was still to come.

"Ed, I've got something to tell you. I got my visa sorted today. I feel like I've got so much more to do there. I'm going back. I'm going back to Brazil."

And that was it - his decision was made. It was remarkable how easy he made it sound.

And yet strangely, by the time he delivered the news, it barely felt like a surprise. Despite having waited too long to be back in touch with David, and now him being *there* right beside me, in almost every other respect I now understood that he wasn't *with me* at all. He was in a different place, riding a wave that I couldn't catch. *Brazil* – *God* - it was all so far removed from what I'd been doing. Anything could happen to him now.

The best I thought I could hope for, was for him to sprinkle me with whatever he'd discovered and make me hungry in the same way he was. But I would not have long for this to happen. He told me that he would be leaving the following week.

It was a conversation that only served to reinforce my belief that I'd been missing out - that I needed to make up for lost time. But as I suspected, any sense that I could simply forget my previous phoney life without contest or consequence would soon be dispelled. Anyone who has attempted to make that same walk out of darkness, will tell you that it seldom happens that easily. The Devil tries to obstruct you, to tempt you back - to tell you it's impossible after everything you've done. Over the coming days, I'd see this play out in very different ways.

In the short-term, David's example did stiffen my own resolve to put up with the awards ceremony the following evening. It was the only thing really standing between me and my long awaited return to church that Sunday. I was still uptight about it. I spent most of the taxi ride there, feeling conscious that the knot on my bow-tie betrayed my inexperience at such formal events. But overall, I was determined to approach the night positively, having persuaded myself that it would be stuffy and uncomfortable, rather than trialling in any more serious way.

I ran into Bernie pretty much as soon as I walked into the venue.

"Edward, hi," he said, while shaking my hand in a fairly warm fashion.

Whether he was genuinely less tense now that he was out of the office, or he had worked-out that he had better be nice to me given that we were going to be in each other's company tonight, this was as affable as I'd known him for a while. During the next five minutes, he did less talking at me in the way I'd become accustomed, and actually asked me questions about myself: how I was enjoying my job at the moment; what I saw as my next career move. He even made a small joke about his grumpy office persona. It was a refreshing change to what I'd become used to.

This exchange hadn't lasted long however, when we were interrupted by someone calling towards us from over his shoulder.

"Bernie, I thought that was you. How nice that you're here?" came an assertive, posh voice.

Bernie introduced the tall and rather pointy featured lady who had wandered over as Veronica Pooke, the Chief Creative Director of Morgan-Harris advertising agency. Like many of the people there, she was an ex-colleague of his, from year's ago.

"Nominated for anything this year?" she asked.

Straight away it was obvious that it was a question asked more to prompt us to turn it back on her, rather than because she was really interested in our response. Morgan-Harris could loosely be described as a competitor to our own agency, but typically dealt with clients that were much higher profile than those we worked for, and was likely to be up for several awards tonight. I could only imagine that manufacturing an opportunity to explain this to us, was a cheap way of asserting that superiority. Recognizing this, Bernie answered the question in a round about way, and tried to land a counter blow by arguing that the awards hadn't reflected the most innovative advertising in recent years. In truth, it was a rather weak deflection.

"Oh Bernie, I really have to disagree. And I must say we've been able to attract the very best new talent to the agency," she said, referring to their previous achievements.

I tried hard not to make hasty judgements about people, but Veronica was fairly easy to dislike.

It was something of a setback then, when she also turned up at our table for dinner. I hadn't really taken the time to assess the other names on the seating plan as we walked through to the rather grand main hall, so it was quick thinking rather than planning, that allowed me to find a spot safely away from her and Bernie.

Perhaps as I'd hoped, the conversation during the meal seemed to fracture into two. On the opposite side of the table, Bernie, Veronica and some fellow industry old-timers talked intently to each other – possibly still boasting about their agencies, or reminiscing about days gone by. I found myself amongst a much younger group. What I hadn't counted on was their eagerness to talk 'shop' every bit as much as the others. They took it in turns to spout off about their agencies and careers, each one trying to outdo the last with descriptions of their impressive responsibilities. I looked around the table to see if anyone else was finding it as nauseating as I was, but it seemed I was alone in my aversion to it all.

I was glad to be temporarily away from Bernie - and particularly Veronica, but I was also particularly pleased when the award presentations began to put an end to the bluster at both ends of the table.

The ceremony itself was hosted by the chairperson of the judging panel, who was possibly as dour and uncharismatic a person as they could have picked. Aside from the descriptions for each category being beamed impressively onto a giant white screen at the opposite end of the hall, he did very little to build up any of the awards, which at least meant we got through them at a fairly brisk pace. As expected, Morgan-Harris was among the first agencies to be recognized. Veronica clearly enjoyed her moment as she strode up to collect their prize for advertisements supporting a brand of vitamins. On returning to the table she spent several minutes admiring the glass ornament she had been presented with - thrusting it in front of Bernie and commenting, "Oh what a beautiful thing - how lovely."

Despite the odd irritation such as this though, I eventually allowed myself to reflect that the night might prove bearable after all. We soon only had two awards left and I knew that when they were done, I could quietly slip off knowing that my departure wouldn't seem premature to anyone bothered enough to notice. Of course, the award category that my work was nominated for was one of those remaining, and the thought of this was also enough to sustain my interest.

I didn't expect to win. Bernie had told me we wouldn't. But as the announcer finally said, "And our penultimate presentation this evening is the award for the 'Household and Domestic' category," my heart started beating a little faster. It was impossible not to mentally rehearse walking to the front, just in case.

But rather than hearing the result declared, there was suddenly nothing; only darkness.

It was like listening to a tennis match on the car radio, only to lose the reception at match point.

Someone towards the back of the room let out a fairly half-hearted squeal and a piece of cutlery clanged against the tiles below, presumably having been dropped. And then after a few moments more, there was a shout of, "power cut," to confirm by then what most people in the hall had already realized.

"I can't see anything," said another voice even more obviously, as the noise level grew again.

Before long an army of waiters emerged, moving methodically among us lighting candles. It was clear that the awards would have to succumb to this temporary interruption.

With the initial commotion beginning to give way, a young girl with red hair on my side of the table addressed everyone else.

"A bit spooky, isn't it?"

"You're right dear, it's very spooky," responded Veronica, enthusiastically.

I agreed. The darkness had the effect of segregating the different tables as if they were poorly lit vessels dotted around a port at night, while the candle lighting dragged and exaggerated the shadows menacingly over the ceiling above. As the seconds passed, you were more inclined to believe that it could go on for awhile.

Veronica was keen to build on that mood even further.

"I know, let's have a séance," she instructed. "Everybody join hands."

It wasn't an idea that everyone immediately embraced — there were as many groans as there were comments of support — but ultimately the whole table did as they were told. I was one of those following orders, but immediately I knew I was doing something I shouldn't. In fact it felt entirely wrong.

"What exactly are you going to do, summon the disgruntled spirits of previous runners-up?" one of the guys quipped in, nodding towards Veronica's award.

"Hey, if it's bitter advertising professionals we're after, there are enough in here already without calling on the departed," said another chap beside me, under his breath.

Not really paying attention to them, Veronica hushed away the jokes and demanded everyone's full concentration.

"Listen, this hotel is over one-hundred and fifty years old, don't you think there are a few ghosts around here that we can invite out for our entertainment? Now be quiet," she said bossily.

She closed her eyes and began.

"Restless spirits are you there? If you are among us, make yourself known — come to us."

Someone else giggled, but with less confidence now. Veronica's seriousness had the effect of subduing them.

"Spirits we implore you to give us a sign that you're here," Veronica went on.

In contrast, with each passing second, I found myself wanting to make it stop even more. It wasn't particularly that I expected Veronica to be successful in communicating with the dead, it was more a matter of principle.

You see, this was the way it always happened with me. So often in my life I'd just gone along with things, and slipped into sin almost by accident. This time I wanted that to change. This was the sort of opportunity I'd been waiting for. I needed to start standing up for myself — standing up for God.

"Listen, I'm out," I said, breaking the chain.

"*Out?*" said Bernie in a slightly embarrassed tone, perhaps hoping he'd misheard.

The man next to me began sniggering under his breath.

Seeing this as a slight against her having instigated the activity, Veronica immediately demanded an explanation.

"What's the matter, we were just getting started?"

I didn't answer.

"Oh come-on, if you're going to be such a spoilsport, you should at least tell us why?" she said, not letting go.

Her tone was confrontational, bullying even, but I wasn't intimidated by it. In fact, now I had gone this far, I felt ready to go further – to explain my reasons if I had to.

"I just don't want to do it. I can just go and grab a drink at the bar, while you carry-on," I said, breathing more steadily now, but feeling dissatisfied eyes upon me from all around.

Their silence demanded more.

"Okay, if you really need to know, this stuff seems creepy and odd to me. No, its more than that – I think it's wrong. I guess it's a religious thing. Seriously, you just go ahead – I'll go."

"Religious?" asked Veronica, still pursuant.

"Yeah...you know, Christian. I'm a Christian, and because of that, it's just something I feel I shouldn't be doing."

"Seriously Bernie, where did you get him from?" she scoffed, prompting a shrug of the shoulders from him.

Though suspecting how mixed-up and unconvincing it had come across, there was something I found pleasing in what I'd said. It felt like swinging a weapon I'd forgotten I had. Sadly, I knew immediately that I hadn't earned the same positive response from all the others. Though most of them were probably just pleased to feast on the humiliation I'd invited, not really caring about my justification, a few amongst them appeared more genuinely irritated. Their faces were screwed-up and disapproving, as if I'd told an inappropriate joke.

As they sharpened their knives, only one person offered any words in my defence.

"Let's just leave it and do something else," said the red-haired girl.

But her appeal was brushed aside.

"No offence chap, but it was only a bit of fun. It's a shame your Christianity doesn't allow that?" said one guy, between sips of wine, while at the same time rolling his eyes.

"Now come on, I'm sure Edward didn't mean to make us all feel so uncomfortable," said Veronica unkindly.

By now even Bernie had begun trying to catch my attention from the other side of the table, slashing his finger across his throat as if to beg me to put an end to the awkward situation that I'd created.

Half of me wanted to just get away, but there was another part which burned to tell them more, to explain my reasons more compellingly.

Just then though – as abruptly as they had failed – the lights returned, reuniting our table with the rest of the room. And as if the brightness instantly washed their minds of what had happened during our time in the darkness, my opponents immediately turned away, back towards the large screen.

I couldn't forget what was happening so easily; I wasn't finished. I was still trying to come to terms with the unjustness of it all. And for this reason I was a few seconds behind them. Only slowly did I turn back and begin reading what was now being projected there: a brand of air-freshener I had come to know well; the name of my employer; and underneath the words 'Winner,' in large flashing letters.

I was still piecing it together, as the host tapped his microphone and began speaking.

"Well everyone, it seems the gremlins have deprived us the element of surprise with this one, but could the representative for this campaign come up to collect your award."

Bernie was already bounding purposefully to the front, looking happier than I'd ever seen him before. I truly was forgotten.

I didn't waste any time feeling annoyed at Bernie for what happened afterwards. He'd obviously hijacked a moment of recognition that was more rightfully mine, but I had reached the point where I was happy for him to have it. I'd taken the next day off as a holiday and I also knew the fact that he'd collected the award probably meant that this, rather than the commotion I'd caused over the séance, would dominate his debrief to the other agency staff back in the office.

For me, the events during the power cut were far less easy to forget. On one level I felt a strange sense of satisfaction, pride almost, at finally having made the pronouncement of faith I'd been running from. And yet, their response also triggered a realization that has stayed with me since. If I was serious about my life with God, I simply couldn't go on taking the path of least resistance, always hoping to conform with those people around me. For the first time in years I'd seen some of the misunderstanding and fear of Christianity that had made me start hiding my faith in the first place; that made Jesus warn us of the division that such convictions would inevitably effect.

"Do you suppose that I came to give peace on earth? I tell you, not at all, but rather division. For from now five in one house will be divided: three against two, and two against three" (Luke 12:51-52).

The difference now, was that rather than hide, I had found myself wanting to explain – as unprepared for it as I was. Perhaps for that reason I remember thinking that I might finally have thrown off my tired charade, and that my own compass might be moving away from the world towards Him. Was I developing a new robustness?

I didn't realize then, but that Sunday would provide another perspective, where on that dial I was.

I was looking forward to seeing Sam again, and also counting on him. I knew I couldn't expect things to be exactly the same as before with the church, and with the guys – David's visit had shown me that. But amid the uncertainty, I could only imagine Sam being Sam. I was relying on him to be a sympathetic link to my past, particularly as he had been through this with me once before, when we returned to the church group after several months away as teenagers. I hoped that because of this he would understand. The rest was down to me - and God. After all, it was the same God I was going back to.

But when Sunday finally arrived, it was Sam who provided my first uneasy moment of the night. And I can only imagine that it showed on my face when I opened the door, as for a moment I just stood there trying to come to terms with the difference in him. He spoke to fill the silence I'd allowed to develop.

"Hello mate; the three musketeers back together again eh?"

It wasn't any one thing about his appearance, but a combination. He had lost weight. His shoulders looked narrower than before and his arms thinner. And as he leaned towards me, not quite hugging me, but patting my shoulders tenderly, I noticed a frailty about his movement. It *was* the same Sam – the same captivating smile – but a pained aspect cut across his brow.

My mind turned back to his illness. Though I was concerned when I first heard, I had almost dismissed it as a consideration since. I wondered whether I should acknowledge the obvious deterioration in him, and ask what had happened.

But on the way to the car and during the journey, it was as if he was doing everything to distract me from that train of thought. He spoke about the church and some of the people I would meet there. He repeatedly told me how great it was that we were back together. He promised that we wouldn't lose contact this time. In all of this he was talking up the prospect of happier times ahead, and diverting attention from the recent past.

And if I was honest with myself, this was exactly how I'd wanted him to be. Sam had always had the knack of making you feel part of his more optimistic world, and I allowed myself to be encouraged by him.

And what he said next had the effect of sidetracking me from this completely.

"Ed, you remember that church meeting we went to at Wolston Leisure Centre a few years back?" He must have presumed I did, as he didn't wait for my answer. "Well *that* guy – the guy who spoke that night – would you believe I ran into him again? He was there one time…at the new place in Rugby. His name's Danny. You know who I'm talking about, right?"

I leaned forward from the back of the car to show I was listening and to urge him to go on. It felt like he was about to slot a large important jigsaw piece into the puzzle of my life.

Sam explained that the preacher, Danny, had been there to support a local Christian rock band who were at the church to perform. He said he'd been determined to introduce himself; to tell him he'd been there all those years before; to see if *he* might remember it even.

"Well he did remember," Sam confirmed. "And you know what else he told me about that night? It was actually one of the first times he'd ever preached. Apparently he was almost overcome with nerves. You'd never have guessed it would you? Anyway, we've sort of kept in touch since. The band - *The Commandments* are playing in Birmingham next week, and he's speaking afterwards. I was thinking we should go? I mean only if you fancy it."

To hear this tonight of all nights was astonishing. Yet at the same time it felt somehow fitting that it would come out as well; as if Sam anticipated perfectly what I needed from him. It also suggested, it *had* meant something special to him back then, just as I'd suspected at the time. I dared to believe that this was a sign that my life was coming full circle to where I'd left off.

Of course, I fully intended to go with him the following week, but I was also gaining confidence that it meant tonight was the start of it all. As we arrived in Rugby, my fresh sense of expectation provided an antidote to my nerves.

The church itself was a modern building, set within a fairly affluent housing estate, and certainly unlike any other that I'd visited before. Its most distinguishing feature was a large glass atrium towards the front, which had the affect of opening up the interior to people passing by on the street. One of the parishioners would later explain, "It's because we want them to see what's going on – so they can choose to join our worship." Most of the people were congregating in this space as we walked in, and judging by the faces of those who looked up, the sight of David and Sam was a welcome one.

They were clearly very popular there, and for different reasons, especially so tonight. Without prying into the details, several people came up to ask Sam how he was after his illness, and news of David's trip meant that he was the focus of attention as well. I knew that the time I'd spent worrying about *them*, and what they would think of me, had been wasted. To some degree I was on the periphery of things, but everyone I spoke to seemed very friendly and hospitable. Briefly, all the complexity I imagined appeared to be lifting.

But then the service began.

It is difficult to pick out one particular moment that made it all feel so foreign. If the church meetings I'd known before were set around a familiar format and rhythm, by comparison this was like a piece of jazz, sporadically throwing up twists and surprises, and each section merging seamlessly into the next. What I do know is that my unease was fairly constant. It was only the immediacy of it that altered; growing and then receding almost with the tempo at which the musicians played their instruments from the front of the room.

The strumming of their guitar strings and pounding of tambourines signalled an initial period of chaotic worship. I was stunned by how quickly the people there seemed to get into a feverish spirit of praise, with many heading directly to the aisles to dance; skipping up and down and waving their arms like novice ballerinas. Others jigged and fidgeted on the spot, while holding their hands up demonstratively in the air. I had experienced and enjoyed meetings where people had sung, clapped, and played music before - of course I had - but this was more intense somehow. Despite thinking that I should join in, my self-consciousness soon drowned this thought, and I became a tense and awkward onlooker rather than participant.

Eventually the singing and dancing did stop, and was replaced by prayer. This wasn't though, the opportunity to quietly gather my thoughts that I might have hoped for. Instead, many of the people there began calling out loud; lots of voices competing and intertwining; making powerful proclamations and speaking in tongues. It created a powerful communal atmosphere that was again unlike anything I'd experienced before, which made me think that these people must be true agents of God. I secretly longed to pray too, to ask God for reassurance, but for some reason didn't feel entitled to in this company. What if one of them was empowered by God to answer on His behalf? What if they decided to help me – singling me out in front of the rest?

I wasn't prepared for that. Increasingly what I wanted was to retreat, merge into the background, escape even, despite feeling a sense of shame for it. What was wrong with me to feel so lost in my Father's house like this?

From then until the end, the meeting continued to be unpredictable, incorporating practices and styles of worship that were all equally alien to me. The climax of this and of my personal crisis, was when one of the leaders began laying hands on several people who had gathered towards the front. As the music continued in its haunting cycle, one by one, they began tumbling bizarrely to the ground, as if they had been overcome or made unconscious even. I wasn't sure which, but I'd long reached the stage whereby any intrigue or interest to understand, had been overtaken by an instinct to leave.

It was then that I noticed Sam looking across towards me. He sat two or three seats away, and had leaned forward, smiling apologetically as if to show his frustration that he couldn't intervene somehow. Until now, it had felt like an entirely personal struggle, yet, he had the look of someone who was bearing all the discomfort inside of me as well. It was a genuine moment of friendship and compassion that would stay with me, but it had come too late to save that night. By that point the damage was done.

Happily for me, the meeting came to an end soon afterwards.

I sat quietly in the back of the car on the way home, leaning my head against the window and resting my eyes shut. The noise of the engine together with the swishing of cars and streets rushing by on the other side of the glass drowned out David and Sam's conversation up front. Perhaps they thought I was napping, or even praying, but either way I was spared having to talk.

For that reason I didn't move from that same position right up until I heard David stop the car outside my house.

"I'll call you guys," I said as finitely as I could, while at the same time moving out of the car. I knew I was vulnerable to being asked what I'd thought of the meeting.

Instead of that, David simply wound down the window and asked, "You okay buddy?"

I just nodded.

I would wish I had taken the opportunity to tell them how I was feeling later - to discuss what I'd seen and heard with them - but at that moment I wanted to be alone.

I'd only walked three or four strides however, when I heard one of the car doors open again and footsteps on the gravel behind.

"Ed wait," Sam called after me. "You seemed a bit quiet back there – you okay?"

"Yeah fine – I mean it was maybe a little different to what I've been used to, but -"

"I can see that – crap! I'm sorry. We did the wrong thing taking you there. I can see how it might seem a bit *full on*. I was exactly the same when I first went."

"Yeah, maybe. It can't just be about me though, can it?"

He paused for a second before speaking again.

"Mate, I know this wasn't your cup of tea, but *The Commandments* next Saturday - come with me, won't you? It will be just like before."

"That would be good" I replied, nodding again, while for some reason noticing how frail he looked again.

The truth was, at that point, I really didn't know whether I was being sincere about going with them or not.

It's often the case that memorable journeys are laced with some frustration. The most rewarding walks normally include an unexpected ascent or headland that seems to appear out of nowhere, just as you believe you are approaching your destination. At such moments a sense of hopelessness and injustice can all too quickly threaten all optimism you have gathered in, and tiredness fills your legs like lead weights.

I didn't blame anyone at the church in Rugby for how I was made to feel that night, and I have never done since, but it appeared that Sam may have been right — going there probably wasn't the right thing for me. Just when I thought returning to some sort of Christian fellowship was within my grasp, now every year, every month and every day that I had been away seemed to count against me and my previous Christian upbringing was worth nothing.

The trouble now was that I was actually left wondering whether I knew where I was really heading at all, as if I'd become disorientated at the worst possible moment. I looked at myself and considered whether my relationship with God had simply become something that was entirely personal to me. Or worse still, that my own beliefs were no longer recognizable to other Christians; somehow altered or blemished having been concealed for so long. It was genuinely a lonely place to be.

I realize now, of course, that it was just the wrong spiritual experience at the wrong time. I need not have felt so embarrassed about how I'd reacted. For many Christians, all the elements that I had seen are normal and instinctive parts of worship - gifts from God; but just because this is the case, it didn't make my own faith any less valid. The Bible contains many examples of where Jesus' followers are rendered similarly afraid and helpless by spiritual events and experiences that they did not understand, like when John sees the form of Jesus in Revelations 1:17.

But perhaps there is another point here. Whenever I've thought about this in the years since, one thing that has struck me is whether it should have been quite so hard. After all those years of bouncing chaotically around in sin, I needed a soft landing.

What I got was something else. It was like an insight into what it might be like to look in at Christianity through a non-believer's eyes. And having known even a fraction of their misunderstanding and fear, I could understand why they might want to disprove it - stop it - to crush it even.

I firmly believe Jesus would have his church reach out to everyone - not only by allowing them to see inside - but by making the worship accessible to them as well. It is perhaps for this reason, that in Corinthians he reminds us:

"Let all things be done decently and in order" (1 Corinthians 14:40).

It is probably also the reason that He challenges the Pharisees and the scribes for hanging onto traditional customs and rituals for their own sake, knowing that these things could also be a barrier to man entering His house:

"All too well you reject the commandment of God, that you may keep your tradition" (Mark 7:8-9).

Those men and women who best serve God stand firmly and unashamedly at the heart of the church, yet at the same time effectively communicate to all men with His good news. They are not apologetic for their faith, they don't tone-down their praise just because the world looks on, but they appreciate that moving from non-belief into belief - darkness into light — is the biggest, most courageous step of all, and ensure that those who have made this transition are received appropriately.

David called me the following Tuesday, having arrived in Brazil. It had only occurred to me having returned home after the Church meeting that I would not see him again ahead of his trip, and I was happy to have the opportunity to wish him well, having been deprived of this by all the chaos of that last night together.

I also knew David would be worried about what had happened.

There was a slight delay on the telephone line, which made what was said between us more a series of marooned statements rather than a normal conversation. However, the requirement to listen and wait intently to David before responding, also seemed to add weight and poignancy to his words. Having told me a little about his journey and the place he was staying, it wasn't long before he turned his attention to me.

"Edward, the main thing I wanted to say was, 'stick with it' — Jesus wants you to." It was the same strange and almost familiar way David had referred to Him before, but this time it felt something of a privilege to have this message relayed back to me in this way.

There was another pause, before the next part came.

"And also, to ask you to look after Sam. Ed, you know he was ill?"

"Ill?" I replied.

"Ed, he had quite severe pneumonia before Christmas."

I instantly felt so stupid and selfish for not having found this out, and being so focused on myself.

"He didn't want to make a fuss. But mate I called him just now, and it seems they're a little worried that some of the symptoms are hanging around. I think he's back with the doctor tomorrow. Ed, I just thought you should know."

Rediscovery

"And I say to you, ask, and it will be given to you; seek, and you will find; knock, and it will be opened" (Luke 11:9).

I don't believe anyone finds their way to heaven accidentally; just as I don't think that anyone misses out simply by choosing the wrong door from a corridor of different options. Despite all the religions and all the doctrines - all the theories for the meaning of life - I'm pretty sure that when you are presented with the truth, deep down you know it. It ultimately comes down to a choice between 'yes' and 'no,' and you either find the courage to walk up to that door and knock, or you begin pretending to yourself that you never really noticed.

The thing is though, once you have knocked – you've knocked.

No matter how long it took you to do it, regardless of what happened until that point, once you have done that, you can expect that door to be answered. The Bible is clear about this.

That morning I opened my eyes to find my room strangely illuminated by a soft light creeping in through the gap in the curtains. It was still too early to be daylight, there were no cars shining their headlights on the street outside my flat, and the moon was absent from the sky, but still just enough light mixed in with the darkness in my eye-line to reveal the silhouette of bags and clothes strewn messily on the floor. It gave my bedroom floor the appearance of a rocky lunar

Edward's Choice

landscape.

My radio was also playing. Although it was Saturday, I'd mistakenly left the alarm function set from the previous day and I now realized it was this that had plucked me from my sleep.

Gradually I became cognisant to what the presenters were saying.

'Here's your traffic update with Ros...

Thanks, Rob. I'm afraid to say that the extreme weather overnight is already causing chaos out there. The A452 is down to one lane between Birmingham and Leamington Spa. The A428 is completely blocked-off as you pass through Church Lawford towards Rugby. And a lorry is stuck on the A4189 between Redditch and Warwick, with traffic building in both directions ...'

She went on, listing another three or so roads that were similarly shut or obstructed by the adverse conditions.

'My advice is to stay indoors, curl up in front of the fire, and spend the day listening to Radio Blue Sky FM. If you absolutely have to venture out on the roads, please take extreme caution.

This is Ros Jupitus, bringing you your traffic and travel update.'

I climbed out of bed and stood for a few moments with my head poked between the curtains, looking out at the sheet of unblemished snow below. It was *its* pristine whiteness, the light it emitted, that had travelled up to my room. I reflected how exquisite it was; how momentarily you could believe you were seeing it all through a child's eyes again, such was the excitement and intrigue it stirred.

But this was only a temporary sensation. Today, I had so many more reasons not to welcome the scene and I quickly remembered I wasn't a child; I was

Jonathan Young

twenty-six. Perhaps because I felt I'd let so much of my time slip by, even *this* had begun to feel quite old recently.

I collapsed my body back onto the bed, drawing the covers protectively around me in the same movement. On a day that would contain so much that would threaten to break my resolve, it was as if I was reluctant to begin dealing with the consequences of it just yet. I didn't need to think ahead to know this could only complicate things.

Instead I rolled over and closed my eyes even tighter, as if to resist the arrival of dawn.

For now it was still early, I was tired, and there was no reason to be awake.

By the time I stirred for the second time, it was closer to midday than daybreak. I had fallen into a deep sleep and was aware that I'd been dreaming.

It had been the most amazing dream.

For awhile I laid there motionless, feeling giddy and somehow torn, as if part of me was still suspended in the images I'd left behind. Although, the details quickly began bleeding away, only moments before the conversations I'd been having - the people and scenes that had surrounded me, had all been sewn together so vividly, it seemed impossible for them not to be real.

I couldn't recall specifically where it had all taken place, or even what I was really doing there initially, but it was clear that all manner of different people from unconnected parts of my life had been gathered together. I also remembered that there was a prevailing sense of gladness – a happy mood shared amongst us all, yet geared towards me in particular.

Whether it was the members of my own family, friends like David and Sam, or others I knew less well from back at school or work that I had spoken to, they had all treated me with a particular kindness - diffidence almost - like the special courtesy you might afford someone at their birthday party or wedding. Even when I encountered Shaun Rainsforth, who was also there, any fear that he might still be angry at me for what had happened between us at school, was quickly brushed aside.

"Edward, its okay - really. I'm happy now," he'd said. "I'm playing in a band called *The Commandments* and its going well. Edward its great to be here, we've come a long way, right?"

For most of the dream, I'd struggled to understand it. But as it progressed and the video-tape seemed to stutter and slow, the penny eventually dropped: I was the reason they were there. They were there to celebrate the end of my difficult years. While it lasted, I believed my struggle might be over.

But of course, it wouldn't last. My last recollection was of us all riding bikes on a wide path aligned with beautiful leafy trees. The sun was shining and there was a pleasant breeze in our faces, and every now and then, one of the group would accelerate away from the rest before turning their head to acknowledge us, almost as if to signal their appreciation for having been part of it all.

It was this sense that made me think: what if this was the end? What if this were a film, and the exit music was about to start? What if this was the end of some sort of dream?

With that, inevitably, it *had* collapsed around me. I had awoken with my legs still twitching as if pushing the pedals of the bike, and with the most extreme sense of well-being.

As simple as it had been, it was the first time in a long time that I could recall everything seeming right with the world; a feeling I hadn't known since the tide of teenage insecurity had started me out on this confused path in my waking life.

Now, I was genuinely sad to have been taken away. I lay there not knowing whether I had any energy left to swim back towards truth.

I had gone to visit Sam at his parent's house the previous Wednesday, and thankfully the news was much better. His appointment with the doctor had revealed that his current symptoms were attributable to a nasty cold and fatigue, rather that the re-emergence of pneumonia, and his mom assured me he was getting better with each day now. I was both delighted and relieved.

It was just unfortunate that I wouldn't get to see his improvement for myself. Sam had been watching television in the spare room, and his mom had found him sleeping on the sofa when I'd turned-up. Though she offered to awake him several times, I insisted that she didn't, and he wouldn't appear again while I was there.

The plan now was for him to stay there until he'd fully recovered, which from her perspective was a welcome development. The doctor had apparently recommended that he take two full weeks rest, and this arrangement not only meant that she could look after him, but also gave her the opportunity to make sure he was following these instructions.

On the way there, I would have settled for any update that meant he wasn't going to end up back in the hospital. Yet as she explained this, it was impossible not to acknowledge the unfortunate part of it for me. I knew there and then that Sam's period of convalescence would mean that he was unlikely to go to the concert.

It was only because I had pledged to myself not to think about my own situation that I managed to conceal my disappointment. Burdening Sam's mom with the details of my problems would have been unfair – she clearly had enough to worry about with him. Besides, I also knew she wouldn't be able to resist helping me somehow - perhaps asking friends from church who would be going to the concert, if I could tag along with them. After so long, I didn't feel that I was deserving of that sort of assistance; nor did I really want it.

Even so, at the end of our conversation as I'd stood up to leave, she was able to offer me some reassuring words; words that *would* come to have bearing on what I would do.

"Its good the three of you are back in touch with one another. Sam missed you

Edward's Choice

Edward. I said he should just pick up the phone so many times, but he'd always say you'd be busy with other things."

It was a nice thing to say, and there was nothing in how it was delivered to suggest it was made up out of kindness.

"It must seem strange for David to be leaving for Brazil so soon?" she continued.

"Yeah it's a shame; I mean it's great for him, but a shame we didn't get more time. It seems like, right now, everything is happening so quickly with them - changing so much - you know?"

"Really? I'm not sure things change that much Edward."

I stopped and turned towards her, perhaps looking slightly confused by the comment.

"Edward, I'm pretty sure there were times when Sam wished he could go back to those days when the three of you were always together. And I don't think David is any different. But things can move on without taking away from that.

You know David rang me in real state before he left for Brazil, saying he didn't feel right going while Sam was still ill. But I told him to go. Blokes of your age should be getting on with your lives, wherever it takes you, not waiting for each other."

The low that I had experienced immediately after my dream, remained with me for the rest of that Saturday afternoon. I stayed dressed in the wrinkled clothes that I'd gathered from the bedroom floor to have a belated breakfast, and though I was frustrated at being cooped up in my flat, I still couldn't find the motivation to go anywhere.

Of course it was more than just the dream by now. With Sam clearly housebound, and the weather being what it was, the chances of going to the concert myself seemed to be fading as well. And now that I believed he was going to be okay, it was as if I allowed myself to dwell on how cruel the circumstances had been to me.

Every so often I stood up and looked out of the window hoping for a sign that things were changing, but the ice did not seem to be thawing. And though I willed the roads to get busier, the only suggestion that anyone on the street had ventured out lay in some solitary tire tracks in the snow and the odd rectangle of uncovered road where a car had left its parking spot. Most vehicles though, remained exactly where they had been that morning.

In a strange way, part of me was looking forward to my opportunity having passed - to when making it to Birmingham from my house in time for the concert, would not be possible any longer. At least then I could face up to feeling bad about it, without the possibility of still going there hanging over me. Every now and then what Sam's mom had said about not waiting for the others would recycle into my thoughts, and while there was still a chance to go, it gave me the uncomfortable sense that it was still partly my choice to stay away. It bothered me - made me restless; but not enough to change my mind; not in itself anyway. At this stage, I was expecting to let my opportunity slip by.

But then Sam called.

"Ed, it's me," he began. "I'm sorry I missed you the other day, I've just been whacked the last few days."

"Don't be stupid, as long as you're feeling better."

"I am. I think I am," he said — perhaps not that convincingly. "I mean, I'm okay but its boring stuck inside you know. My folks have been great, but it's been boring..."

Ill or not, Sam was far too fidgety and sociable a character to enjoy being in one place, and with the same people, for that amount of time. But if his frustration was to be expected, what he said next did take me by surprise.

"I've had plenty of time on my hands to think though. Ed, I wanted to say that I'm sorry we didn't do more to stay in touch before. Looking back, it's crazy that we didn't. I feel lousy."

It wasn't Sam's nature to dwell on things. He was normally so optimistic - so impatient for the future - that this was one of the few times I'd ever hear him contemplate the past, let alone regret it. From my perspective, it also felt unfair for him to take all the blame for it when clearly we were all equally responsible. I tried to interject to tell him. But as if this had just been the first half of a load he was determined to get off his chest, he continued without any thought of pausing.

"Mate, I'm also sorry about tonight. You know the gig. I feel really bad."

"Don't worry, I've barely thought about it," I said, obviously not being truthful.

"You should go anyway, don't you think? In fact, I thought - well hoped you might already have left to go there?"

"Sam, I don't know. I'm kind of tired myself."

"Ed, listen. That night when we saw Danny before, when he spoke all those years back - well, I'm not sure whether I would have gone back if it hadn't been for you coming with me. I don't want to be the reason you don't go tonight. Mate, please, just think about it will you? I don't want to sound weird, but I've been praying that you might go."

It wasn't as if my mind was made up following this conversation; all the reasons I had for staying at home still stood. But subconsciously it must have had some sort of bearing as I remember feeling a rush of nervous energy, calling me to attention. I found myself looking up at the clock wondering whether I could still make it. And then, as if some deeper unprompted determination had taken over, I was suddenly rushing around my flat, throwing myself in and out of the shower and then getting dressed.

Before I knew it, I was plodding through the thick snow towards the bus stop at the end of my street. With the night closing in and the snow again turning to ice, it still didn't seem sensible to drive but I figured that the bus routes were likely to be passable.

However it had happened, I was soon stepping onto the *'6:45'* into town. I paid the driver and found a seat.

So was this it? Was I finally prepared to defy all the things that had happened to discourage me and step out of the fog of recent years? The truth is, on that bus ride I didn't really know. Even as I sat there, looking at all the other passengers heading out to their own night spent in the city's bars, restaurants or theatres, my head was still spinning with uncertainty. I asked myself: what if somebody that I knew got on the bus now, where would I say I was going? If someone like Jared happened to be taking the same journey, would I dare tell him I was trying to get back to a life with Jesus?

Doing this now, alone, and in the end so spontaneously, felt so odd and in many ways like the most telling example of my undercover Christianity yet — even if I was trying to leave it behind. It made me wonder if I could in fact ever escape it completely.

And with that, my mind turned to finding evidence to the contrary. I began hurriedly tracing my way back through different memories and reference points in my life, believing I might be able to arrive at some sort of summation of who I really was. The decisions I'd made at school, university, and later at work — everything seemed open to reinterpretation. And as if each memory was a slot on a roulette wheel that might wind up determining my future, I knew even now that the ball could come to rest anywhere.

As if to emphasise the point, I was soon standing waiting to disembark the bus at Eltham Street - the closest stop to St. Peter's Church where the concert was taking place — but was already preparing a plan of where I might go if I decided that I couldn't go through with it. I stepped off the bus feeling annoyed and troubled that my doubts still wouldn't die down. If this was what God intended, surely now as I approach such a significant point, I should be more certain?

My route meant briefly cutting through the city centre. I'd lost count of how many times I'd walked along the same roads as one of the pub-goers going from place to place, but tonight was very different. Tonight, I skulked past the pubs and turned my head away from the neon lights that shone out from above their doorways, as if to stop them identifying me. Mingling among the people there, with all their laughter, their drinking, shouting and singing, was like looking back at an old photograph of myself. I felt like I had to get in and out as quickly as I could, before the area could reclaim me. And because I'd once been part of it all, it now seemed much more ridiculous and threatening to me than it really was. Briefly, I imagined Adam and Eve peering back at the sinful world their actions had unwittingly created – confused, frightened, and ashamed.

I turned the corner, away from the busiest area, and onto Clarence Street. There, two hundred feet or so away was the church.

The first thing I noticed was that there was a queue. For some reason I hadn't expected a queue. I quickly surveyed the faces standing there and spotted at least two people that I thought I recognized from all those years before, when I regularly attended such events. They hadn't been friends of mine, but there was no telling if they would recognize me; I knew there was a chance that they would come over to ask how I was and who I was meeting there. What would I say if they did? For some reason, even the prospect of this filled me with a deep sense of dread. And then there was the queue itself. Was I supposed to wait there in line with all the others? Anyone might pass by and see me standing there waiting to go in. Even as I was thinking this, I was still approaching – getting closer. My heart began pounding.

I knew that I would have to make a decision quickly. I needed to commit to it, or get out of there. I could be spotted at any time now, and then I'd be bound to join them. 'Don't look up,' I told myself – 'Don't make eye contact with anyone.' And because of that I knew.

I couldn't do it. I just couldn't do it.

I turned down the last available side road before the church; jerking my body into the darkness - already despising myself. In a split second, anxiety had turned into despair and despair to anger. I had trapped myself forever in the most miserable, hapless state, where I didn't belong to anything, and no-one belonged to me.

Immediately, I wanted to punish myself. I wanted to head out and show my defiance.

Looking back over my shoulder, away from the church, I scanned the street to see where I was and where I might go. It was a narrow road that had a tall gloomy warehouse on one side, and a tightly packed bank of terraced housing on the other. Towards the end of the row there was also a pub. I impulsively headed in that direction.

It was a tired looking building with dirty outside walls that probably hadn't been painted in decades. Its appearance perhaps said something about its keeping, but also added to its sense of durability and importance; you couldn't imagine it ever relinquishing its spot on the city's landscape. Unpolished gold leaf lettering stuck above the doorway spelled out, 'The Black Bull.'

As I entered, I realized that the exterior was a befitting advertisement for the inside. An unpleasant smell that might have been unwashed dishes or the remains of overcooked food filled my nostrils, and ahead of me, I noticed a channel of well trodden carpet being held together by a maze of industrial tape. Despite being a Saturday night, only five or so other customers were dotted around the room. They sat apart, not really talking to one another, and stared sadly into their drinks or at the small television set in the corner.

But none of this mattered to me. I felt too destitute – too abandoned to care about them. At this point I believed that whatever their stories were, they couldn't be as wretched as mine.

The bar-tender, a stout man with an unshaven, angry face and tired bloodshot eyes, approached me. Rather than asking me what I wanted, he simply raised his eyebrows in a way that prompted me to speak.

"Vodka...double vodka," I said immediately.

Edward's Choice

No sooner was it delivered than I'd tipped it down my throat. I put the glass down with a thump on the bar, glancing back over at him to provide a refill, and continuing our theme of communicating without speaking. He snatched it back and walked towards the dispenser, at the same time shaking his head disapprovingly. I knew that to him I was just another drunk to wander in off the street, and that other than collecting my money, he probably had little interest in why I was there. In reality, I wasn't sure that I even understood this myself.

Drinking alone like that wasn't something I had ever done before, or would ever do again. I only knew that I'd wanted to blot out the anger that was eating away at me. I had only just nodded my approval for a second top-up, when the ridiculousness of my behaviour began to hit home. This just wasn't me. Whatever statement I was trying to make to God, to myself – I didn't really believe in how I was doing it.

I knew then that I had to get out of there. I threw down a twenty pound note to cover the price of the drinks, leaving the latest double-measure of vodka untouched on the bar. Drinking it already seemed like the most absurd thing I could do.

It wouldn't be wasted though. As I was walking out I noticed one of the pub's regulars stumbling over, clearly intent on profiting from my profligacy.

So what was left for me now? Despite all the scenarios I'd anticipated on the way there, I hadn't ever arrived at a plan of what I'd do if it came to this. And in all probability, if I could have wished for anything, it would be to have myself transported away from it all, back to my house and into bed. At least then in the following days I could busy myself with work, and other things, and slowly begin to forget that it had happened. Perhaps I'd even convince myself that I could continue with my life as it was before.

Rather than going home though, I began walking back towards Clarence Street and the church. I didn't really know why; I still had no intention of going inside, but for some reason I found a bench opposite and sat down. With my head bowed between my legs, I allowed the cold to travel into my body through my toes and begin to take a grip on me. By now the queue had disappeared inside the doors and I could hear the music of *The Commandments* reverberating from within the large stain glass windows. The lyrics were indistinguishable, and I couldn't decide whether I liked what they were playing, but for a time it felt like the deep base and drums were the only things keeping me conscious.

I didn't know how long this would be the case though. Slowly, it seemed like I was less and less in control of my thoughts, until sleep and the night seemed certain to overcome me.

Instead of this, I became conscious of myself crying - crying and praying.

'God, why is this happening to me? God I have asked to come back, but you are not letting me? Father, please.'

The next thing I recall was the sound of a car stopping close by. My initial thought was that it might be the police looking to move me on, but as I slowly opened my eyes I was reassured this wasn't the case. The vehicle ahead of me was quite small and old, and rather than reflective stripes or police markings, it had fading red paint and a rash of rust that spotted around the wheel arches and doors.

Through the steamed-up glass pane, I could see someone wrestling with the winder to get the window down.

"Edward?" came the voice from within.

It was Trudy. She had been going to the concert as well, and for some reason had arrived there late. The horrid coincidence of it being her to discover me there, sad and alone, just as she had done that previous night in Birmingham, wasn't lost on me. And as with the last time, I instantly felt ashamed at my compromised and pitiable state. If there was any doubt before, surely *this* would make up her mind about what I had become.

Edward's Choice

"Edward, what's going on?" she said. "Edward are you okay?"

I shook my head slowly and dispiritedly, for some reason finding her questions impossible.

But not waiting for me to reply, she heaved the passenger door open, beckoning me to get in.

"Edward?"

"Please, I've been drinking. You really don't want me in the car," I said, mouthing the words, far more than actually making them audible to her.

"Edward please, just get in."

Having done as she had said, I just sat there for a few moments.

"Edward, what's wrong. I want to help you?"

They felt like wonderful words, but I'd convinced myself that I was beyond help. I could only believe that she would soon come to her senses just as she seemed to have done the time before - or perhaps hear the music and realize how late she was. I looked up at the clock on the dashboard.

"I don't care about the concert," she said, guessing what I was thinking. "Ed, please tell me what's happening to you?"

By now tears were welling in my eyes and I could hardly bear to look at her, let alone talk, in case they escaped.

But after a few seconds more, I did talk.

"Trudy, the truth is I'm lost. I'm so lost, that I'm not sure I can find my way back anymore."

And that was all I needed to say. She reached forward pulling my head towards her, allowing me to sob unashamedly into her shoulder. And with each tear-drop, something changed; the weight upon me seemed to lessen.

"You know what Edward; everything is going to be okay."

For some reason, even then, I knew she was right.

I stayed with Trudy for the rest of that night. Soon after she started up the car and began to drive; not to the concert, but into the city centre and to one of the all night coffee shops, where we sat-up talking. I told her everything: about my unfortunate plan to live my Christian life as some sort of secret, the sad deterioration of my faith as a result, and about my apparent difficulty in returning to the church after all that time. I even explained the embarrassing sequence of events that had led me to sitting on the bench where she found me that evening. I seemed to be talking for hours, and Trudy listened in a way that was more intent and earnest than I could have hoped.

And then she began filling me in on the story of her life during the last few years; revealing just enough of her own fallibility and sadness during that period to make me feel less alone. Part of this was her regret at having let me walk away from her that night in town. I was flattered by this, and also relieved. Somehow I'd come to regard everyone at church in such elevated terms, that I expected them to be immune to the disappointments and problems I experienced. To my surprise, she also told me that they had talked about me and even prayed for me at the church group after I left.

Gradually, I let go of the pain and the crying, and allowed myself to feel hopeful. I was reassured that what had happened was real, and wouldn't disintegrate like my dream several hours before. I would have been happy for that night and that feeling to go on forever.

But I also knew it didn't need to.

When we eventually did leave, it was about 5:30am. As she drove towards my house to drop me off, I remember hearing the birds singing. It seemed warmer than the previous day.

I knew that my heart was mending again.

In the End

My life wasn't suddenly transformed following that night – much stayed the same. Briefly, I allowed myself to reflect that I finally felt content, and that was a sweet sensation, but before long the 'ups and downs' that I experienced before, returned in broadly the same proportion as they had always come along. Even when you think you've discovered the right path towards Jesus, it doesn't mean that all your problems suddenly dissipate and happiness ensues; at least not here on earth.

What I did find somewhere in those hours spent with Trudy, was an irreversible confidence that I would never be alone in facing life's difficulties again.

I also found the conviction that I had to tell others what I had learned. Though there was probably very little that was unique about my story up until that point, it is because of this that I've dared to believe that it is a story worth telling.

You see, I'm pretty sure that there are others out there like me. I suspect there are other Christians who have concealed their beliefs through fear of what school friends or work colleagues might think if they knew. Maybe they have not gone so far as to convince themselves they could serve God as secret agents, but in choosing not to show their faith quite as openly as they might, there are likely to have been times when they have been frustrated or led astray just like I was. Think about it - how many people have that same sense of Jesus guiding them when they step out to work or school on a Monday morning, as they did when they were in church on Sunday? To some degree, aren't most Christians out there Closet Christians?

And the thing is, if those years in my life showed anything, it was that it matters. It matters, because all those people that I touched in one way or another deserved a chance to understand what motivated my behaviour; just maybe this would have tweaked their own curiosity about the great truth that I knew. It also matters because, during those most testing periods, like when the presence of Shaun threatened to expose my secret at school, or during my brief relationship with Kate, I know now that I would have made more of the right choices had I been focused on what He wanted rather than trying to fit in with everyone else.

Perhaps the most important reason for living your Christian life without shame or secrecy is because Jesus demanded it.

"For whoever is ashamed of Me and My words in this adulterous and sinful generation, of him the Son of Man also will be ashamed when he comes in the glory of His Father with the holy angels" (Mark 8:38).

Ultimately, the balance I was trying to achieve between acceptance in worldly terms, *and* serving God is the impossible compromise.

That doesn't lessen or make light of my reasons for striving towards this. I know there are many people who frequently experience awkwardness because they *do* choose to be open about their beliefs - Christians who are likely to have noticed conversations strangely stall when they approach, because others censor what they allow the 'Bible Basher' hear. But we cannot expect to inherit heaven and still find total acceptance among non-believers. As Jesus said:

"For what will it profit a man if he gains the whole world, and loses his own soul?" (Mark 8:35).

For this reason, I decided to step out of the closet – I've been trying to be more open about who Edward Hill really is. Even though I'll try not to forget what it is like to look in on the God Squad from the outside, from that night I knew it was time I made clear where I stood.

Of course, I am still a sinner. There are still times when I feel that my behaviour does little to honour Him. The difference now though, is that I try not to let the thought of my sins knock me off course or make me believe that I've been relegated down an imaginary line to heaven. Instead, like in my dream, I imagine cycling towards that better place along with everyone else, to a Father who is keenly waiting for *all* His children to return.

Trudy didn't save me that night. I was saved because I asked God to come back into my life. The question is, will you do the same or will you love the world so much that you hesitate?

What I say to you, is get on your bike.

THE END

All scripture taken from the New King James Version®. Copyright © 1982 by Thomas Nelson, Inc. Used by permission. All rights reserved.

EDWARD`S CHOICE

ISBN 978-1-926625-44-7

© 2010 by Jonathan Young. All Rights Reserved. This book is protected by the copyright laws of Canada. No part of this publication may be reproduced, stored in a retrieval system, or transmitted, in any form or by any means, electronic, mechanical, photocopying, recording, or otherwise, without the prior written permission of the publisher, or under consentual agreement.

Printed in the United States of America at LaVergne, TN for worldwide distribution.

Printed in the United Kingdom at Milton Keynes, England for distribution in the UK.

Revival Nation Publishing
Ontario • CANADA

www.RevivalNationPublishing.com

Lightning Source UK Ltd.
Milton Keynes UK
24 August 2010

158936UK00001B/38/P